Heartwood Hotel

A True Home

Also by Kallie George

Heartwood Hotel, Book 2: The Greatest Gift

Heartwood Hotel, Book 3: Better Together

Heartwood Hotel, Book 4: Home Again

The Magical Animal Adoption Agency, Book 1: Clover's Luck

The Magical Animal Adoption Agency, Book 2: The Enchanted Egg

The Magical Animal Adoption Agency, Book 3: The Missing Magic

Heartwood Hotel

A True Home

Kallie George

illustrated by
Stephanie Graegin

𝕯𝖎𝖘𝖓𝖊𝖞 • HYPERION
Los Angeles   New York

First Hardcover and Paperback Editions, July 2017
10 9 8 7 6
FAC-020093-19084
Printed in the United States of America

This book is set in 15.25 Fournier MT/Monotype, Qiber/Fontspring
Designed by Phil Caminiti
Illustrations created in pencil

Library of Congress Cataloging-in-Publication Data
Names: George, Kallie, author. • Graegin, Stephanie, illustrator.
Title: A true home / by Kallie George ; illustrated by Stephanie Graegin.
Description: First edition. • Los Angeles ; New York : Disney-Hyperion, 2017.
    Summary: Mona the mouse is precisely the maid they need at the grandest hotel
    in Fernwood Forest, where animals come from far and wide for safety, luxury,
    and comfort.
Identifiers: LCCN 2016022969 • ISBN 9781484731611 (hardcover) •
    ISBN 1484731611 (hardcover) • ISBN 9781484746387 (paperback)
Subjects: CYAC: Hotels, motels, etc.—Fiction. Mice—Fiction. Forest Animals—Fiction.
    • Autumn—Fiction.
Classification: LCC PZ7.G293326 Tr 2017 | DDC [Fic]—dc23
LC record available at https://lccn.loc.gov/2016022969

Reinforced binding
Visit www.DisneyBooks.com

*To Luke: Home is where the heart is,
and my heart is with you.*
    —K.G.

For Theresa and Sophia
    —S.G.

Contents

MONA THE MOUSE

Home is where the heart is, or so she'd heard. But Mona the mouse had never had a home—at least not for long. A dusty hay bale, an abandoned bird's nest, a prickly thicket—in her short life she had lived in more places than she had whiskers. And now her latest home, an old hollow stump, was being flooded out by the storm.

When she'd found the stump in the summer, with a mushroom table already in place and the stream nearby, it had seemed too good to be true. Why had no other animal claimed it for its home?

Now Mona knew. She watched, perched on a

root in the corner, shivering and scared, as the water rushed in, swirling around her bed made of moss, lapping at her table, threatening to wash away her suitcase.

The suitcase was all she had left of her family. It was made from a small walnut shell and had a tiny heart carved on the front. Mona reached for it now.

Time to move again, she thought with a heavy sigh as, holding the handle tightly, she waded out of the stump and into the storm.

Rain beat down on the trees of Fernwood Forest, which were just beginning to turn the colors of fall. Instantly, Mona was soaked—from nose to tail. Her paws sank into the wet ground with every step.

Which way should I go? she wondered. To the right was a farm, but it was very far, and it had a cat. She knew because she had once tried to live there. So it was either to the left or straight ahead.

She was about to go straight when . . . *CRACK!* Lightning flashed and Mona jumped. To the left it was, then. She headed deeper into the forest, hopping from twig to leaf, trying to stay out of the mud.

If only there were a rock to burrow under, or a clump of mushrooms, or a hollow tree. But there wasn't. There wasn't even a sign of another animal. *Everyone else must be hidden away in their homes,* Mona thought, *safe from the storm.*

Soon rain was collecting in her ears. She shook

the droplets of water out of them, but it only helped her hear the frightful storm more clearly. The wind whistled, whipped, and whirled—and brought with it the sound of howls. *Wolves!*

Mona squeaked, quickening her pace. The wolves howled again. They sounded far away. But wolves were wolves, and any small animal was scared of them. They were hunters and not to be trusted. Nothing was worse than wolves.

The rain fell harder still. Is this how she would go—like her parents, swept away by a storm? If only she had a paw to clutch, or someone to tell her everything would be all right. But she was alone.

And then, at last, Mona spied something: an enormous tree, rising so high she couldn't see the top of it. And it was hollow! She hurried toward the opening.

But right away she knew this wasn't a home for a mouse. This was a bear's den. No bear was in it now, and likely one hadn't been for a long time.

Still, the faint smell of fur, fish, and berries hung in the air, and she knew she would never be able to sleep soundly there. What if a bear *did* come back? Although she wasn't as scared of bears as wolves—she had lived near a bear for a while, and it had been more interested in eating berries than in eating her—she didn't relish the idea of being trapped in a den with one.

So, reluctantly, Mona scurried out, back into the storm.

A stream, swollen by the rain, blocked her way. She looked for a place to cross. A stick had fallen over it. Mona was good at balancing—all mice were—and she was almost across when she looked up and saw, in the dark bushes ahead, eyes!

The glowing eyes of wolves! She was certain. Not just one pair, or two or three, but so many that Mona couldn't even count them. Her heart leapt into her throat while her paws slipped from the stick and . . .

Splash! She fell into the water.
Whoosh!

Just like that, instead of by wolves, she was swallowed by the stream, which gulped and gushed and carried her away.

Water filled her mouth, and she coughed and sputtered. Clinging desperately to her bobbing suitcase, she was swept along by the current down a hill, past bushes and ferns and rocks and roots, deep into the forest.

Farther and farther the stream carried her. She scrambled up onto her suitcase and watched as the trees grew mossier and more and more twisted. *This must be the heart of the forest,* she thought—somewhere she had never been.

At last, the stream slowed into a pool made from some large roots. One root reached forth like a helpful paw, and Mona grasped it and clambered out of the water.

She gasped. There in front of her rose another enormous tree. This one, however, was more than enormous. It was . . . *majestic.*

Giant branches fanned out around the top like a crown. Golden leaves blocked the rain and wind. In between roots, moss grew so neatly it looked as though someone had tucked it in and trimmed it to fit. Maybe someone had . . . for in the trunk, just above her head, was a carving.

It was a heart, like the heart on her suitcase, but in the center of this heart were the initials HH.

What could it mean? she wondered.

Mona couldn't resist. Slowly, she reached up on tiptoe to touch the carving.

CLICK.

The heart pressed inward, and a door in the trunk swung open.

THE ACORN FESTIVAL

With a squeak of wonder, Mona stepped inside to warmth, light, and the delicious smell of roasted acorns.

The room was large—very large for a mouse—big enough for a group of small animals to gather. Across from the door was a stone hearth, unlit but decorated with a garland of colorful leaves. A mossy rug lay in front of it, surrounded by a couch and chairs made of twigs, which were lined with more moss. To the left stood a large wooden desk with a big book and twig pencil on it. And from the ceiling hung rings of candles, casting a soft golden glow.

Mona had never been in such a fancy place.

Who lives here? she wondered. But there was no one around to tell her.

There was the faint sound of music and laughter, however, coming from behind the hearth. Mona took a few more steps into the room and spied an open doorway near the fireplace. The sound was coming from there. Mona started in that direction, but paused. She *was* a mouse, after all, and she had to be careful. She sniffed cautiously.

The smell of roasted acorns was stronger now.

Surely animals who ate roasted acorns weren't a threat. And then, out of the corner of her eye, she noticed a sign above the hearth. She hadn't seen it before because it was half covered by the garland of leaves. She could just make out what it said:

WE LIVE BY "PROTECT AND RESPECT,"
NOT BY "TOOTH AND CLAW."

Relieved, Mona followed her nose and ears through the doorway, down a short hallway decorated with more garlands, and to another door— a much larger one with a plaque on it that read BALLROOM. It was slightly ajar, enough so Mona could slip through.

Inside was another marvelous sight, and a much more lively one! Rabbits, chipmunks, squirrels, hedgehogs, birds! Even a lizard. And largest of all, a badger! Not muddy or wet like her, but dressed up and dancing, eating and laughing. Mona clutched her suitcase tightly and looked around in awe. She had only ever encountered a few animals at a time in the forest, never so many all in one place.

Against one wall was a table stacked with food: mushrooms, juniper berries, licorice roots, and acorns—oh, the acorns! Mashed, steamed, fried, souped—so many types that Mona didn't recognize many of them. And in the center of the table, a giant honeycomb with cups beside it to scoop out honey to drink.

Not far from the table, above a small stage, was a banner—THE FIRST ACORN FESTIVAL: CELEBRATE AUTUMN'S ARRIVAL—and on the stage, three beautiful dark blue birds crooned. Their song came to an end and the room filled with applause.

"Thank you. Thank you!" said one of the singers. "We are the Blue Bow Warblers, and we're honored to be singing our final concert here before our flight to the south. We're happy so many of you could make it, despite the storm. And now, though it is raining outside, we can make it sunny in here with one of our favorite melodies, 'Moon Shine, Sun Rise'!"

More applause filled the room, and whistles and cheers, too. As the birds burst into another tune and the dancing started again, Mona's mind raced.

Were all these animals staying here? Where had they come from? Her thoughts were interrupted by a voice.

"Hello, Miss Mouse." The lizard stepped in front of her and gave a short bow. "Were you searching for help at the front desk? My apologies. My name is Gilles. How may I help you?"

Mona noticed he was wearing a bow tie around his neck, and a large key, which was made of wood and had a heart-shaped top. He was exceedingly clean—a glistening green, as though his scales had been polished—and he seemed hesitant to get too close to the muddy puddle that had collected on the wood floor around Mona.

"I . . . I . . ." stammered Mona.

"I am afraid we are full tonight. Booking for the Acorn Festival took place months ago. Why, we were overrun with messenger jays bringing room requests. You should have sent one yourself."

Mona found her voice: "I didn't know. I've never been here before. Where . . . where am I?"

"Where are you?! Why, Miss Mouse, this is the Heartwood Hotel."

"What is that?" asked Mona.

"Only the finest hotel for forests around!" exclaimed Gilles. "The Heartwood Hotel has roomed such guests as the speed-race champion Randolph the rabbit and the duchess squirrel Henrietta the Third. It has hosted the wedding of the richest skunks in the forest and boasts festivals for every season. Not to mention its reputation for rest and relaxation." The lizard's tongue flicked in and out as he continued. "Why, no other spot can guarantee protection from wolves, coyotes, and cougars. 'Sleep in safety, eat in earnest, and be happy at Heartwood.' That's Mr. Heartwood's motto—one of many, actually. Please don't tell Mr. Heartwood you haven't heard of us. He will blame the *Pinecone Press*. They have yet to review us. Reviews of French hotels, reviews of Italian ones, but of Heartwood? None as yet."

"The *Pinecone Press*?" said a booming voice. "Is this the elusive reviewer at last?" Joining them at the door was none other than the largest animal in the room, and perhaps the oldest, too, Mona guessed from the stoop of his shoulders. It was the badger, with glossy black fur and a smart jacket and vest. Not just one, but an entire set of wooden keys hung around his huge neck.

Mona trembled. Badgers were not always kind to mice, and this one gazed down upon her with a particularly stern look.

"Oh no, sir," said Gilles. "This is not the

reviewer. This is Miss . . ." He paused. "I don't believe I caught your name."

"Mona," she said.

"Miss Mona is here for a room, but I've told her we're booked, Mr. Heartwood, sir," said Gilles.

"Ah, I see." The badger sniffed, his great nostrils fanning out wide.

Mona swallowed hard. "Oh, please, I have no place to stay. My home was washed out in the storm. Please. I . . . I think there are wolves out there."

"Not nearby, certainly," huffed the badger. "We never see those beasts in this part of the forest. They live in the Great Woods, beyond the Fernwood Foothills."

"No, they weren't nearby," replied Mona. She had seen the wolves before the stream had carried her away. Had that been in the Fernwood Foothills? She didn't know the parts of the forest and what they were called.

"I see," the badger said again, twirling the white whiskers on the sides of his cheeks. His gaze caught her suitcase and he peered closer. "A heart. What a coincidence." He looked back at her intently.

"I've always had it," said Mona. "It belonged to my family."

"And where are they now?"

"I lost them a long time ago in a big storm like this. . . ."

"You did, did you?" Mr. Heartwood tugged his whiskers, his eyes concerned. "And so storms strike, not once, but twice . . ." He looked like he might say something more, but he simply gave his whiskers an extra-hard tug and then looked back at the party and glanced down at the floor, which was messy with bits of food. "Ah, crumbs. We have more than a few. A night for a night, that we could do. You're a small sort of helper, but an extra paw is an extra paw. Gilles, make it be. Take her to Tilly."

Then, with a nod and a toothless grin, Mr.

18

Heartwood returned to mingling with the guests.

"Well, I say." The lizard's tail twitched.

"What did he mean? I don't understand," piped Mona.

"Mr. Heartwood will let you stay for the night if you are willing to clean up after the party with Tilly, our maid. Probably mentioning the wolves helped. Mr. Heartwood has a soft spot for any small animal in trouble, and he especially dislikes wolves. His wife was taken by them, you know, while she was on a journey to visit her sister. That's why he started the hotel: to create a safe place for animals, especially traveling ones, to stay. But sometimes I think he forgets that it *is* a hotel, not a safe haven for every wet whisker that comes by. Of course I don't mean any disrespect to you, Miss Mouse. In any case, you'd better come with me."

"Oh, thank you," said Mona.

"Don't thank me yet," said Gilles, opening the door wide. "You haven't met Tilly."

TROUBLE WITH TILLY

Mona followed Gilles away from the party and back into the lobby, to a candlelit staircase near the stone fireplace. She could see that it went up and down many floors.

"Come, come." The lizard gestured to her. "Tilly will be in the kitchen."

The lizard led her down to the floor below and along to the end of a hallway. Gilles pushed open a swinging door to reveal a room smaller than either the lobby or the ballroom, but still bigger than any of Mona's old homes.

The kitchen was filled with even more delicious

smells than the ballroom. Baskets of nuts and berries hung from roots on the ceiling over a long table that was cluttered with pots and bowls, spoons and serving trays. Cupboards were dug into the dirt walls; some were open, showing stacked dishes and jars of dried seeds and herbs of all kinds. A sink, made from a large shell, was filled with dirty pots and pans. There was a fireplace in a corner, and over it hung a pot, bubbling with acorn mash.

A plump porcupine was stirring the mash with a particularly long quill. She wasn't alone. A red-furred squirrel with a very bushy tail sat at the table,  nibbling at a giant puffy cake.

"Don't poke your paws into everything, Tilly, dear," chided the porcupine. "There's got to be enough for Mr. Heartwood. You know how hungry he gets after a party."

"Yes, Ms. Prickles." The squirrel reluctantly pushed the dish away. "But after the party . . . that's when I have to clean up. I won't get a chance to eat anything."

"I'll set some seedcakes aside for you, dear."

"I like acorn soufflé better," muttered the squirrel, just loud enough to be heard.

Soufflé? That must be the name for the puffy cake, thought Mona.

"It's for the guests—you know that," replied the porcupine, turning around and shaking her stirring quill at the squirrel, only to catch sight of Gilles and Mona. "What's this? Gilles? Who have you brought us? Not a guest, surely."

"Of course not," replied Gilles, as though offended by the suggestion. "She's a new maid— Mona. Mona, this is Ms. Prickles, our cook."

"Hello, dearie," said the porcupine.

"And this," continued Gilles, gesturing to the squirrel, "is Tilly."

Mona stuck out her paw.

But Tilly didn't take it. Her tail bristled instead. "New maid?"

"Just for the night," continued Gilles. "She will help you clean up after the party. In any case, they're Mr. Heartwood's orders, not mine. He wants you to help her find the brushes and an apron."

"A mouse? Help? Mice are too small to be maids." Tilly's tail bristled up even more, bigger than her body. "And she can't help anyone clean anything. Why, she's just tracking in more mud!"

"Your problem, not mine," said Gilles, heading out of the kitchen, but not before the porcupine said, "If you're going back upstairs you might as well bring up the soufflé, before Tilly eats it all."

"I'm the front-desk lizard. It's not my job to serve the food," grumped Gilles, but he took the soufflé anyway and, with that, disappeared.

Tilly didn't even protest the departure of her favorite dish. She was still glaring at Mona with such ferocity that Mona couldn't help but tremble.

Mona looked down. Her paws *were* still very dirty. "It was the storm . . ." she muttered.

"Oh, dear, dear. You poor thing," gushed Ms. Prickles. "Now where is a nice rag?" The porcupine opened a cupboard under the sink and rummaged through it. She pulled out a rag that looked like it was made of soft bark. She handed it to Mona, who quickly rubbed her paws and even her tail.

"There, that's better, isn't it, dearie? Mona, right?"

Mona nodded, handing back the towel.

"Such a sweet name, for such a sweet little thing. You know, I think I've still got a bit of my cheese crumble left. Would you like a nibble? It's a favorite with our mice guests."

At this, Tilly broke in, "No time for eating.

The party will be over soon. And now I have more work to do, showing her around. . . ."

"Oh, Tilly—hush, tush," said Ms. Prickles. "Show a little sympathy. I'd think you would, considering . . ."

Tilly went completely silent. There was a long pause, but Ms. Prickles didn't say anything else, except for "Oh, Tilly. It's been a long day for all of us, hasn't it?"

"Yes, Ms. Prickles," said Tilly finally.

Ms. Prickles turned to Mona and explained, "Mrs. Higgins, our housekeeper, is sick with a cold, and it's meant double the work. And with the party going on . . . Well, it's not easy to keep a hotel this size running, that's for certain."

"I can usually do it by myself just fine, except for this feast," replied Tilly with a humph. Then she looked at Mona again and sighed. "Well, we'd better get you an apron."

"You can have the crumble later, dearie," Ms. Prickles said to Mona, as Mona once again was led away.

After dropping off her suitcase in Tilly's room ("I guess you'll have to share with me," she said), they passed more rooms and hallways and at last reached a storage room, where Tilly dug out a broom, dustpan, and apron. The apron was much too big, so Mona wrapped the strings around her waist several times before tying them. It was so long she hoped she wouldn't trip on it.

"Do I need a key?" asked Mona, pointing to the one that Tilly wore around her neck. After all, Gilles had been wearing one, too. And Mr. Heartwood had lots.

"Pah," replied Tilly. "You're only working the night. Keys are for proper staff, like me. You'll just be cleaning the ballroom."

Just the ballroom, indeed!

With only a few guests left, nibbling the last of the buffet, the ballroom was far larger than it had seemed before. And far messier. Crumbs of seed-cakes and bits of mushrooms and acorns dotted the knotted wood floor. Mona had to sweep up all the crumbs with a broom—a dried dandelion turned upside down. Like the apron, it was too big for her, but she held the handle down low. She dumped the crumbs in a bucket, even though she was so hungry she wanted to eat them.

And there was honey everywhere! Tilly gave her a rag and a nutshell of soapy water, but the honey was very hard to scrub off.

It was a long night, especially since nothing Mona did seemed to be good enough for Tilly. "Still sticky," she'd say in between doing her own tasks, and she'd make Mona return to the spot and scrub some more.

Through it all, the storm raged, the wind rattling

the shutters of the ballroom. Mona was grateful to be inside and warm, despite the hard work. Hard work, but how full of marvels! The bright clusters of elderberries that Tilly took down from the ceiling. The instruments on stage, made of reeds and seedpods, that pinged and tinged when Tilly moved them. The woven willow-strap slippers left behind by a guest. And best of all, the sunshiny yellow leaves that Mona helped Tilly arrange in acorn vases on the tables, to greet the guests in the morning.

The night ended with a bite of cheese crumble, too. So, when Mona lay down in Tilly's room on the spare bed of feathers—the most comfortable bed she had ever had—Tilly's loud snores didn't bother her. (Tilly sounded grumpy even while sleeping!) Mona wasn't grumpy, though. When at last the little mouse fell asleep, her dreams were filled not with fears of the forest, but with the wonders of the Heartwood Hotel.

Pledging a Paw

It was with a heavy heart that Mona, suitcase in paw, followed Tilly down the hall to the kitchen the next morning. It was time to leave. Time to go back out into the forest to search for a new home.

Tilly, on the other hand, seemed much more pleasant now, and full of chatter.

"I have been here for years. This was my fifth Acorn Festival. Thank goodness the skunks didn't come this year. They did once. Now *that* was bad. Lord Sudsbury never learns to leave his stink at home, no matter *how* many times Mr. Heartwood has told him."

"Skunks stay here?" asked Mona.

"Oh boy, do they. They come every year for their anniversary. I always fix up their room 'specially for them. But that's not for a few weeks. I've got the squirrels' rooms to prepare first. It's their big convention—on best nut-storage practices. Since I'm a squirrel myself, only I can say this . . . but they're trouble. They party all night long."

"Oh," said Mona.

"Not that it matters to you, of course."

By this point, they had reached the kitchen. The big table was laden with food: bowls of seeds and honey, and plates of fried thistles. Around the table sat Ms. Prickles and Gilles, as well as animals she hadn't met, even a woodpecker. Mr. Heartwood sat at the head of the table.

"A party of fun, well-planned, now done," Mr. Heartwood said, raising his cup. "Good job, everyone."

Mona didn't have a cup to raise, and didn't even know if she was supposed to stay for breakfast. Mr. Heartwood had, after all, offered only one night and one meal. She didn't think breakfast was part of it, even though the seedcakes smelled really good—toasty and buttery. And familiar, too. Had she eaten some, long ago?

"Aren't you having breakfast, dearie?" said Ms. Prickles, interrupting her thoughts. "Try a seed-cake. It's my own special recipe."

Mona shook her head. "I probably should leave now. . . ."

"That's right," said Tilly as she squeezed in between two rabbits.

"But you need to eat! Especially if you have a long way to go," said Ms. Prickles. "Where is your home, dearie?"

"My home was washed away in the storm," said Mona.

Ms. Prickles's forehead creased. "Oh my. And what of your family?"

"I don't have any," said Mona in a quiet voice.

"Oh. Oh, dear. Tilly, do you hear that?"

Tilly's tail bristled up again.

"That was a bad storm," commented one of the rabbits. "Good thing it's over, so the guests can leave. Imagine if they were stuck here . . . it would be a disaster! It's already too busy."

"Hmm," said Mr. Heartwood, staring hard at Mona. "It *is* our busy season. And we are understaffed, what with Mrs. Higgins under the weather. If you pledge your paw to our hotel, and give it your all, you may stay for the fall. You will receive a salary of Fernwood farthings, too, of course."

Mona couldn't believe it.

Tilly looked shocked, too.

"So, Miss Mouse?" said Mr. Heartwood. "What say you?"

"Oh yes!" said Mona. "I mean, I do." She put her paw on her heart.

Mr. Heartwood nodded. "Good. Now take a seat. After all, work begins when stomachs sing."

"Yes, sir!"

And so, after leaving her suitcase by the door (she would return it to Tilly's room after she ate), Mona found a place at the table, between Ms. Prickles and Gilles. It was half a spot, really— much too small for most animals—but for Mona, it was just right.

Tilly Gives a Tour

"Humph, hiring you without Mrs. Higgins's approval. She won't like that," muttered Tilly after breakfast, as she reluctantly showed Mona around.

"Who's Mrs. Higgins?" asked Mona, her stomach full of the delicious seedcakes.

"The housekeeper. I told you that already. She's sick, remember? You have to listen better. There's a lot to learn around here. My mother always said mice had brains like Swiss cheese—full of holes."

"But . . ." started Mona. She had felt happy but now her stomach sank. She knew that wasn't true.

"But nothing. Just try to keep up, okay?"

Tilly pointed to a closed door across the hall from the kitchen. "That's Mrs. Higgins's office. After breakfast the first thing you have to do is see her. She'll give you a list of the guests who are checking out, the guests who are checking in, and who has requested room service. If a guest is checking out early, you start cleaning that room first. Most guests arrive in the early afternoon. All their rooms must be ready. Beds made, sinks and bathtubs scrubbed, soaps out, and treats on the pillows."

Mona nodded, wishing that she had a notebook to write it all down.

"How long has Mrs. Higgins been sick?" asked Mona.

"Since the end of summer," said Tilly. "The summer was stressful. First the Strawberry Festival was cancelled because the strawberry season came too early, and then we couldn't have a Blackberry Festival because the blackberry season never arrived at all; it was too dry. The summer really never has had a successful festival yet, according to Mrs. Higgins, and she's been here since the Heartwood's start. Then there were the frogs."

"What about the frogs?"

"They purposefully overflowed the tub in their suite, and it took Mrs. Higgins and me half a day to mop up the mess. We were damp from our heads to our tails, and she caught a bad cold from that. Not me, though." Tilly pointed to the door of Mrs. Higgins's office. "Look, she's posted my schedule."

Pinned to the door was a piece of paper with writing on it, which Tilly took down and showed Mona.

- Breakfast tray for Branch Room 2
- Breakfast tray for Twig Room 10
- Hot honey cup for Twig Room 6
- Extra soap for Root Room 3

"That's for the boars' suite, no doubt," said Tilly knowingly. "They like to scrub twice."

After room service came the check-outs, which took up half the page. But there were only two check-ins.

"It's going to be a busy day with all the festival guests leaving," said Tilly, folding up the list and tucking it in the pocket of her apron. "You better not slow me down. Come on, there's lots more to show you. We only have an hour." She pointed to another door down the hall, which was propped open. "That's the laundry room, where bedding and bath towels are cleaned and sorted, and where we pick up most of our supplies. Guests can have their clothes washed here, too."

Mona peered inside. Wet sheets hung from racks to dry and the room smelled like soap. There were tubs of steaming water, as well as different-shaped bins of all sorts of bedding. Already the two rabbits from breakfast were crumbling up the leaves in one of the bins. They waved to Tilly.

Tilly waved back, then said to Mona, "Different guests prefer different sorts of bedding. Rabbits like dried grass or oak shavings. Squirrels like crumbled leaves and twigs. Birds like nests of moss, and moles dirt and some leaves. Some guests have special requests. There are bags there, to carry the bedding in." Tilly pointed to some large sacks hanging from pegs on the wall. "You fill them with what you need."

Tilly moved on to the staircase and pointed down. "The floor below is the root floor, where there are rooms for rabbits, moles, voles, shrews, and ground squirrels. Farther down are the hibernation suites and food storage, and below that, Mr. Heartwood's quarters." But Tilly didn't head down, she headed up. Mona hurried after her.

In the lobby, Gilles was at the front desk, bent over some papers. He gave Mona and Tilly a nod, then returned to his work. Tilly gestured to the hearth. "We don't light that till the First Snow Festival."

"What's the First Snow Festival?" Mona asked, but Tilly didn't reply. Instead the squirrel nodded to the sign that read WE LIVE BY "PROTECT AND RESPECT," NOT BY "TOOTH AND CLAW."

"Everyone staying at Heartwood has to abide by that rule. Mr. Heartwood is very particular that all guests meet his mandates. Like the Six-Legged Rule. They're so small—everyone would have to constantly watch where they put their paws."

"What's the Six-Legged Rule?" asked Mona.

Again Tilly didn't answer, rounding a corner to show Mona the dining hall ("for guests only"), which was beside the ballroom, before hurrying on to the second floor.

This floor was dedicated to guests' enjoyment. There was a games room, a library, and a salon. And then it was up to the guest rooms. The trunk floors were for bigger animals, like skunks, hedge-hogs, and badgers. ("But we've never had a badger except Mr. Heartwood stay here.") The branch floors were for squirrels and chipmunks and other smaller animals. ("Our most frequent guests.") The twig floors, higher up, were dedicated to birds. ("And opossums. They like hanging-branch balconies.") And then, near the top, were the biggest and most expensive suites: the honeymoon suite and the penthouse suite.

"Oh, it must be so nice to sleep in one of the fancy rooms," murmured Mona.

"Don't be silly!" cried Tilly. "The staff never sleep in the guest rooms. We always sleep downstairs."

"I was just imagining . . ." started Mona.

Tilly snapped, "Keep up. There's only one place left to show you."

At last, they came to the top of the staircase.

"This is the stargazing balcony," said Tilly. "It's especially popular at night."

Mona followed Tilly out a doorway and stepped outside onto a balcony built on top of a giant branch, with a wooden railing all around it. It was filled with tables and chairs and couches, and it had the most fantastic view Mona had ever seen. "Go on," said Tilly, sitting in one of the chairs. "You might as well take a look."

Mona leaned against the railing, careful of the binoculars that hung there, and stared out.

The blue sky stretched up all around her, and the treetops waved below, a sea of green and orange and red. Golden sun was peeking up in the distance. "Oh!" breathed Mona. She had never been up so high, not in all her life. She felt like a bird.

And, in fact, there was a bird on the balcony, too.

It was a beautiful swallow with glossy blue feathers and a starry white breast. Although she was the

same size as the Blue Bow Warblers, she seemed much smaller. One of her wings was in a sling, and she was staring out toward the sun. A drop of water—was it a tear?—slid off the bird's beak.

"Are . . . are you okay?" asked Mona.

The swallow turned her head to the mouse. There were tears in her eyes. She really was crying. "What was that?" the bird said in a sad, small voice.

"Oh, nothing. Sorry to disturb you, Miss Cybele," Tilly said, suddenly by Mona's side. "Mona, come on!" she whispered through clenched teeth.

"You are not supposed to talk to guests!" snapped Tilly, once they were back on the staircase and heading downstairs. "That's another rule. Unless of course a guest talks to you first. I thought you would know that."

"But she was crying. . . ."

"And now you're trying to make excuses!" huffed Tilly.

But Tilly didn't get any further. She was interrupted by a bigger huff. Up the staircase, huffing *and* sniffling, hobbled a very round, very gray hedgehog with a handkerchief in one paw and a cane in the other.

"Oh, Tilly, *there* you are! What are you doing?"

"Don't get mad at me, ma'am," said Tilly. "It's

Mona. She's the new maid Mr. Heartwood hired. He told me to show her around."

"New maid?" Mrs. Higgins blinked at Mona, puzzled, then let out an explosive sneeze. She wiped her nose with her handkerchief and shook her head. "I'll find out all about you later," she said to Mona, and then to Tilly, "But there's no time for that now. Lord and Lady Sudsbury are coming. In fact, they just arrived!"

THE SKUNKS' STAY

"The skunks?" cried Tilly. "But they aren't supposed to arrive for weeks!"

"Yes, the skunks, but please call them the Sudsburys, Tilly," said Mrs. Higgins sternly.

"Sorry, ma'am," said Tilly.

"They decided to come early," continued Mrs. Higgins, "for what reason, I am not sure. But they are in the lobby as we speak. Mr. Heartwood is meeting with them. With all the festival guests still here, he is concerned about their scent. You know Lord Sudsbury. He's so high-strung. Mr. Heartwood simply does not want him to spray. If he sprays . . .

Well, you know how long it took to get rid of the smell last time. Luckily no one complained, but rumors could have started. . . ." She sighed. "I am not sure what good a lecture will do. But that is not our problem. You must prepare the honeymoon suite at once for them. They plan to have breakfast in the dining hall and check in at noon."

"That gives us lots of time," piped Mona, but she instantly wished she hadn't.

"Perhaps with a regular guest's room, but these are the Sudsburys!" cried Mrs. Higgins, punctuating her sentence with a sneeze.

Tilly nodded and gave Mona a smirk.

"Here's the list," said Mrs. Higgins, handing Tilly a slip of paper. Mona had to stand on tiptoes to get a peek. It read:

Special Requests:
- Black-and-white striped sheets
- Marinated mushrooms

- A skunk cabbage bloom
- Perm rollers for Lady Sudsbury
- Tie press for Lord Sudsbury
- Binoculars

"The binoculars are new," said Tilly.

"What are they for?" asked Mona.

Tilly rolled her eyes. "It's none of our business."

"There are some extra pairs on the stargazing balcony," said Mrs. Higgins. "Ms. Prickles will bring up the mushrooms. I'll take care of the room service this morning. Hurry, scurry," she said. "No mistakes. You know how particular the Sudsburys are."

"Don't worry," assured Tilly as the hedgehog bumbled down the stairs, "I'll take care of everything." She turned to Mona. "Come on. We need to get supplies. You heard Mrs. Higgins. No mistakes."

Although Tilly didn't say it, Mona knew that

meant her. So it was with a nervously twitching nose that she followed Tilly downstairs and back up again with supplies—bigger ones for Tilly and smaller ones for herself—to one of the fanciest suites in the hotel.

The honeymoon suite was beautiful, with a curved-branch balcony and a bed in the shape of a heart. "It's stuffed with the fluff of cattails," explained Tilly. "It's the best bed in the hotel. But don't get any ideas about trying it out." There was a hollowed-out burl for the tub and a desk twisted from twigs. In the corner of the room stood an enormous pinecone decorated with candles, and paintings of happy animal couples hung on the walls. There was even one of a pair of mice!

Mona couldn't help but stare at it. She had never spent much time around her own kind.

"So how did you lose yours?" asked Tilly, gesturing to the picture.

"Lose what?" replied Mona.

"Your family . . ."

"Oh," said Mona. "It was a long time ago. I don't really remember them. I wish I did. What about your family?"

"That's not your concern," said Tilly briskly. "Sweeping the floor is. I'll change the sheets."

Tilly handed Mona the smaller basket of cleaning supplies and a new apron, with pockets, which she put on. It was plainer than Tilly's and still a little big, but at least it didn't drag on the floor.

Swish, swish, swish. She swept the wooden floor with a broom, even around the tub, being careful not to miss a single speck of dirt, and wondered why Tilly had gotten so mad. It was Tilly who had asked Mona about *her* family, after all. *She* hadn't started the conversation.

Tilly's voice broke her thoughts. "What's taking you so long? Ugh, let me do it. You go fetch the skunk cabbage from Mr. Higgins."

"Is that Mrs. Higgins's husband?" Mona asked.

"Of course," said Tilly. "He's the gardener. But no more questions. Just go down to the lobby and along the hallway, past the ballroom, to the back door. You can't get lost."

Mona wasn't so sure, but Tilly took the broom from her and said, "Hurry!"

So Mona scampered down the staircase, through the lobby, and past the ballroom. As Tilly had said, the hallway continued, ending in a large door. The doorknob was way above her head. But then she saw a smaller door built into it. *This must be for guests who are small like me,* she thought, opening it.

Outside, the sun was no longer peeking out from the trees but parading in the sky, though the air was still cool. Everything smelled fresh from the big rain. In front of her was a large courtyard surrounded on three sides by a wall of blackberry vines. Leaves were heaped in one corner, as though they had been recently piled there. The dirt ground had been swept, and there were several chairs made of twigs, for guests, surely.

On the right side of the courtyard, in the vine-covered wall, was a gate that said FOR HOTEL STAFF ONLY. Mona headed there. She pushed it open and stepped into the garden.

On one side a stream wound its way through banks of roots. *It must be the continuation of the one that swept me to the hotel,* Mona thought. With all the water, it was no wonder the tree had grown so large. And the water made for a healthy garden, too.

There were wild strawberries and blueberries and ferns. A large huckleberry bush rose from the side of a log. Onions and artichokes were in one patch together, and in a shady bed were different types of delicious-looking mushrooms. There were clovers, dandelions, and herbs, too—chives and oregano, and one plant that overpowered all the rest with its fresh, sweet smell: peppermint.

She breathed in deeply. "How nice," she sighed.

A portly hedgehog with a pair of tooth-sharp shears poked his head out from behind the plant. "Isn't it, though?"

Mona jumped back, surprised. "Oh!"

"Don't worry," said the hedgehog. "I'm Mr. Higgins, the gardener. And you . . . Wait, I remember you from this morning. You're the new maid."

Mona nodded.

"And partial to peppermint. Oh, no need to look upset. I love the plant myself, but some guests have complained that the smell overpowers the courtyard, so I need to trim it back. Here, why don't you take some?" He held out a sprig.

Mona smiled and put it in one of her apron pockets.

"You can have more, if you'd like," he said.

"Thank you. Maybe later," said Mona. "Right now I need a flower from a skunk cabbage."

"For the Sudsburys, I assume?"

"How did you know?"

"I grow it especially for them. They like a flower in their room because it reminds them of home." Mr. Higgins led the way down to a swampy area near the stream.

"Stay back," he told her. "You don't want to get your paws muddy. . . . There it is," he said, pointing to a leafy plant that towered above their heads. "The skunk cabbage." In the center of the plant grew a few stalks. Only one, a small one, had a yellow flower on the end shaped like the flame of a candle. It was about as tall as Mona.

"Skunk cabbage doesn't usually grow in the fall, but I always cultivate one for now, though typically I plan to have it flower in a few weeks' time. Luckily there's one blooming early." Mr. Higgins ducked under the leaves, wielding his shears. *Snip*. The flowering stalk wobbled. Mr. Higgins caught it and called to Mona, "Take one end. I'll help you carry it to the door. We don't want it dragging through the dirt."

Mona did as he asked. The flower was heavy, but she was able to keep it off the ground. When they reached the door, Mr. Higgins let go of his end.

"Can you manage from here?" he asked.

Mona nodded. "I think so."

"Best hurry up," Mr. Higgins said. "Don't want to keep Tilly waiting. Don't let her give you grief, though. She's been through a lot, but that's no excuse."

Mona nodded again, surprised.

Then Mr. Higgins gave her a wink and headed back into the garden.

Holding the stem carefully, Mona dragged the flower down the hallway and into the lobby. Two shrew guests, chatting near the hearth, gave her an odd look as she pulled it around the couch and up the staircase. The stairs were hardest, and she was careful to go slowly so as not to damage the flower. By the time she reached the honeymoon suite, her limbs ached.

The room was sparkling clean. The rollers and the bowl of marinated mushrooms were laid out on the desk, and the tie press sat in a basket on the freshly made bed. Binoculars hung from a hook in the doorway to the balcony. "Lean that flower against the pinecone," ordered Tilly.

As Mona struggled to do so, Tilly continued, "Then scrub the tub. That's all that's left. I'm going downstairs to eat. I've done my share. It's not *my* fault you're so slow."

But I had to get the flower. You asked me to, thought Mona. She remembered what Mr. Higgins had said, that she shouldn't let Tilly boss her around. Still, she kept her thoughts to herself. She didn't want to risk making Tilly grumpier.

Instead she picked up a scrubber while Tilly strode out of the room, her bristly tail giving the doorframe a final dusting. "And by the way," she added, "they'll be here any moment."

With that, Tilly was gone, leaving Mona alone with the tub. Any moment? How would Mona ever finish in time? She had never cleaned a tub before. If she had, she would have known that she didn't have to scrub the outside, but that's what she did. She had only just started on the inside, using her cleaning basket as a stool to help her climb in, and was polishing the taps when the door opened. At first she thought it might be Tilly returning, but an instant later, she knew it wasn't.

"There, there, my petite perfumery. No need to fret any longer. Here we are at last, and it is time to relax."

Mona crouched down low, her whiskers trembling.

It was the skunks!

The Big Stink

Mona's ears twitched as she listened, barely daring to breathe.

"See. There's everything here you like, darling."

"The binoculars? Where are the binoculars?"

"Right here, my sweet aroma."

Steps crossed the room, and Mona could hear the door to the balcony being pushed open. "Do you think it's safe out here?" came Lord Sudsbury's voice.

"You know the balconies are private, dear," said Lady Sudsbury. "And well hidden by branches. Mr. Heartwood thinks of safety above all else."

"If you're certain . . ."

The suite was silent for a moment, and Mona imagined Lord Sudsbury gazing out through the binoculars, across the treetops.

What should I do? Mona wondered. *How long will they stay in the suite? What if they spend all afternoon here?* She had to keep working. There was still lots to do in the rest of the hotel, but she didn't want to suddenly show herself. They were guests and she wasn't supposed to be in their room. Not to mention that if she surprised them, they might spray. And then she'd be in *big* trouble.

"Oh, come, please, darling, put those down. You won't see anything from here. We're up too high, and very far from home now. Try to forget. . . ."

"Forget?" cried Lord Sudsbury. "When I know wolves are in the forest? And not just one or two, mind. A whole pack! And more are gathering, Rose!"

Wolves! Mona remembered them from the night of the storm. Were more really gathering?

"Oh, Hawthorne, you're always worrying about something," continued Lady Sudsbury. "Wolves, coyotes, foxes . . . even spiders. And that's why I booked us here for an extended stay. There is nothing to harm us at the Heartwood Hotel. Wolves do not even know where it is! We are safe here, Hawthorne."

"Safe? SAFE?!"

"Deep breaths, Hawthorne, deep breaths. You are working yourself up again."

"I am not!" cried Lord Sudsbury. Mona could hear him pacing. "It's not like YOU heard the howls. It was ME who woke up that night. I heard them!" His footsteps grew louder and louder. Mona knew Lord Sudsbury was in the bathroom now.

"And I CAN'T forget them, no matter WHAT you say. It wasn't YOU who—ACK!"

Mona looked up at a very handsome, very

distressed skunk. He was wearing a black-and-white striped tie that matched his fur. His tail shook.

Mona opened her mouth to explain, but too late. . . .

WHISH!

Lord Sudsbury sprayed. The smell instantly filled the room, and the tub. Mona pinched her nose but it barely helped. She gasped and choked.

"Oh, Hawthorne!" murmured Rose. "You just HAD to spray, didn't you? And after what Mr. Heartwood said. Now we will have to leave. So much for safety. So much for relaxation . . ."

"It was just a little!" cried Hawthorne, who tugged at his tie. "Rose, I didn't mean to . . . but look!"

Lady Sudsbury's steps grew louder as she walked into the bathroom.

"A mouse!" she gasped, looming over Mona.

Lady Sudsbury's black fur was curled and tied with tiny white bows, while her white fur was

brushed smooth and sleek. Her tail shook and Mona
thought she, too, might spray, but then she cleared
her throat and her tail stopped shaking. "Who are
you?" she demanded.

Mona slowly stood up, pinching her nose. She
tried not to tremble as she looked up at them.

"I'b the maib," she said.

"The what?" asked Lord Sudsbury.

"I think she's the maid, my darling," replied
Lady Sudsbury.

Mona unpinched her nose, the terrible aroma
overwhelming her again. She tried to ignore it as

she continued quickly. "Yes. I'm the maid, and I was just finishing cleaning the tub when you arrived. . . . I'm so sorry."

Lord Sudsbury stared sadly at her, twisting his tie in his paw. "It's too late now. . . ."

"It's my fault," said Mona.

"It is your fault, indeed," said Lady Sudsbury stormily. "I expect you will explain everything to Mr. Heartwood."

"Of . . . of course . . ." stammered Mona, her heart sinking.

But to Mona's relief, Lord Sudsbury quickly said, "Oh, don't make her, Rose. What if Mr. Heartwood asks *us* to leave? It was me who sprayed, after all. I can't bear to go home now, when we've just arrived."

"But the smell . . ." she replied. "The other guests and Mr. Heartwood are sure to notice even with this little bit. It's too powerful."

Powerful. Mona had heard that before, and it gave her an idea. The peppermint! It was powerful smelling, too, but sweet and fresh. And Mr. Higgins said she could take some.

"I . . . I think I can help," said Mona.

"What do you mean?" asked Lord Sudsbury.

"Just wait right here," she said as she climbed out of the tub. "Open the balcony door and fan the air. I'll be right back."

Before leaving the room, Mona rubbed herself all over with the sprig of peppermint from her pocket. It didn't get rid of the skunk's smell completely, but it definitely disguised it. Then she hurried back to the garden for more.

Mona's plan worked. She and the Sudsburys crushed peppermint and stuffed it around the tub and under the bed—and even hung sprigs all over the pinecone—and when they were done, the mint masked most of the skunk odor. Lord Sudsbury was very grateful, and Lady Sudsbury's glower softened. "It smells a little like home," she said. And though it smelled nothing like a home Mona would want, she felt better—better enough to scurry away to have a bath (telling Tilly that she was dirty from the cleaning, which was sort of the truth). "Well you'll have to miss lunch, then," said Tilly, sniffing at Mona suspiciously. Mona nodded and hurried to the washroom.

She ran a bath and scrubbed well, using a soap that was shaped like a little heart. The bubbles smelled like nuts and honey and made her think of cozy nights and full bellies.

If she had a home, this was just the way she'd like it to smell. She sank into the warm water and, for a moment, felt as pampered as Lord and Lady Sudsbury (*though*, she thought, smiling to herself, *much more relaxed*).

Miss Cybele's Song

As the days passed, Mona got to know the hotel and its routines.

Still, there was a lot to learn. She left her duster in a room once, and another time forgot to put out acorn cookies on a pillow. But soon enough, and with very little supervision, she was cleaning rooms all by herself.

Mrs. Higgins was still too sick to spend much time with Mona, but now every morning Mona had a list of rooms pinned to the office door with one of the hedgehog's spines, which looked almost like Ms. Prickles's quills. Once Mona made the mistake of calling the hedgehog Ms. Prickles. Mrs. Higgins sternly reprimanded her, and Mona learned just how dissimilar the two were. Luckily, she was saved from further lecturing by a sneeze.

"She needs a good rest," said Tilly. "How could you think she looks like Ms. Prickles?! Humph!" There were no sneezes to save Mona from Tilly.

Tilly, however, was strangely quiet and distracted when the squirrels—fifteen, from different parts of the forest—arrived. Their convention was certainly distracting. During their meetings in the ballroom, the squirrels were serious, but as soon as the meetings were over, they drank lots of malted honey, which led to flying squirrels soaring down the stairs, nut-cracking competitions, and—once—balcony jumping, which Mr. Heartwood was *not* pleased with. Mona and Tilly had to clean up the squirrels' messes. One time Tilly even left her own duster in a room. When Mona rescued it, Tilly was actually nice and thanked her. But it didn't take Tilly long to return to her usual self.

One night, Tilly asked Mona if she was ever going to unpack her suitcase. When Mona confessed that there was nothing inside, Tilly laughed and said, "Good. Then you won't have anything to pack up when you're let go." Mona tried to laugh, too, though the words stung. She wished she could say something, but she wasn't quite sure what. She had never had to stand up for herself before; she'd always been on her own.

Was Tilly alone, too? Mona had never seen her write a letter, or receive one, though many of the other staff did. Ms. Prickles had so many relatives that she was constantly getting small deliveries—letters and special herbs to cook with. Maggie and Maurice, the laundry rabbits, were, in fact, sister and brother. But Tilly never mentioned any family, and Mona was afraid to ask. Ms. Prickles gave Mona her only clue.

After a particularly tough day with Tilly, Mona

was sitting in the kitchen having some licorice tea and seedcakes. She was reaching for her fifth seed-cake when Ms. Prickles chuckled.

"Oh," said Mona, pulling back her paw. "I'm sorry. I didn't mean to eat so many. I didn't realize . . ."

"No, no, I take it as a compliment, dearie. But tell me, is something the matter?"

"It's Tilly," Mona confessed.

Ms. Prickles sighed heavily. "What has she done now?"

"Nothing, exactly . . . She's just so . . . so mean to me. All the time. Everyone else is nice. You.

Mrs. Higgins—even if she's stern. Mr. Heartwood. But not her."

Ms. Prickles sighed again. "Don't judge her too harshly, dearie. She's had a tough time, that squirrel."

"That's what Mr. Higgins said, too. But what do you mean?"

"It's not my tale to tell. Nor Mr. Higgins's," said the porcupine. "But remember, everyone's heart has hurts. Some more than others."

Did a hurt allow you to hurt others, though? Mona didn't think so. Still, she wondered exactly what hurts Tilly had. She couldn't imagine Tilly ever crying. Not like Cybele, the swallow who she had seen on the balcony.

Cybele obviously had hurts. No one knew how she had injured her wing. She was very shy and rarely left her room. All Mona knew was that she was booked to stay here for the rest of the fall and the winter, too.

It was growing cold in the hotel now, and one morning Mona decided to ask Mrs. Higgins for a warm blanket for her bed.

Mrs. Higgins was wrapped in a blanket herself, at her desk. Tilly was pouring her some tea while they went over a schedule.

"Of course, Mona, you may have a blanket. Of course," said the hedgehog, dabbing at her red nose with her handkerchief. "And bring one up to Miss Cybele on Twig 44 while you're at it. She put in a request."

"I can do that, ma'am," said Tilly quickly.

"It's best if Mona does it. Miss Cybele is very . . . shy."

Tilly didn't look pleased, so Mona didn't stay to hear any more and hurried out to the laundry room. She found the softest blanket she could and carried it up to the swallow's room. She was about to knock when she heard a noise inside.

Not just any noise: singing. Though she knew it wasn't polite, she pressed her ear against the door to listen.

"Tweet-trrit, chiddy-deep,
Onward, southward, wing to wing,
Here we soar, hear us sing,
Onward, southward, home we go,
Where flowers bloom and warm winds blow."

The tune drifted into a series of lovely *"Tweet-trrit, tweet-trrit*s." Then it stopped.

Mona waited and then knocked, hesitantly, on the door.

A moment later the swallow opened it a crack, just enough to poke her beak out. "Yes?" she said timidly.

"I'm so sorry to disturb you," said Mona, "but I've brought the blanket."

"The blanket?"

Mona held it up. "You requested it?"

The bird nodded. "Oh yes," she said.

She was about to take it in her beak when Mona added, "I heard you singing. It was beautiful."

"Oh?"

"It was . . . better than the Blue Bow Warblers," continued Mona enthusiastically.

Cybele gave a tiny chirping laugh and then, after a pause, said, "My flock liked my voice, too. I . . . I always led the migration melodies."

"Was that what you were singing, a migration melody?"

"Part of one."

"Oh," said Mona, wondering what the rest of it was like.

As though the bird had read her mind, she quietly added, "If you would like, I could sing the rest of it for you."

Mona knew the rules. She wasn't supposed to talk to guests, much less be entertained by them, but the swallow opened the door and Mona couldn't help it. She stepped inside.

She hadn't been in Cybele's room before. Usually Tilly cleaned it when Cybele visited the stargazing balcony. Unlike the other bird rooms on the twig floor, which had birdbaths built into their balconies and many roosting pegs stuck into the walls, this room was bare and small. It didn't really seem like a bird room at all, except that, instead of a bed, there was a nest of twigs, moss, and blankets built up in one corner of the room. There was a single peg on the wall, which looked more like a coat hook than a roosting peg. Below it was carved something that made Mona's eyes go wide: another heart. Just like the one on her suitcase, except this one had an inscription below it:

"It is so nice of Mr. Heartwood to let me stay here," Cybele explained, "considering how few Fernwood farthings I have. Supposedly he's let other guests who are in need stay here before."

"Mr. Heartwood is really kind," agreed Mona as she added the blanket to the nest, wondering who the other guests could be.

Cybele took her place on the roosting peg, so Mona sat down on the moss rug to listen to the swallow sing.

The rest of the song was as wonderful as the first part she'd heard, and when it was done, Mona clapped and Cybele glowed.

"Would you like to hear some others?" asked the swallow.

"Please!" replied Mona.

And so Cybele began another, about the sea, and when it was finished, another about the moon.

"That's one of my favorites," Cybele said shyly when she was finished, adjusting her wing in its sling. She looked out at the sky. "At night, I gaze at the moon and think of my flock. I wish I could be with them."

"What happened?" asked Mona quietly.

"It was the storm, on the day of the Acorn Festival. A gust of wind took me by surprise and knocked me into a branch, and I sprained my wing. I can't fly south with a sprained wing, so I came here. I'd heard about the Heartwood and knew it was a safe place to stay. I hoped my wing would heal quickly, but it hasn't, and now I know I must stay until the spring, though I have barely enough farthings even for this room, especially if it's a long winter. . . . But worse . . . although the hotel is so comfortable and I'm treated well, it's not the same as being with my friends. It's lonely. I'm lonely."

Mona nodded, and added thoughtfully, "I guess I've never really had many friends."

"Oh," said Cybele, looking surprised. "But you

are so kind and friendly. I thought you must have lots of friends."

Mona shook her head. "I've never stayed anywhere long enough."

"What about here?" said Cybele.

"I'm new," said Mona. "I arrived the same day as you. But I do like it here, very much." As the words left her mouth, Mona realized it was true, despite her troubles with Tilly.

"I like it, too, even if I miss my friends. In fact, I've even started to make up a song about the hotel. Would you like to hear it? It's not quite finished, though."

Mona knew she should leave, but how could she resist a song about the Heartwood? She nodded eagerly.

Cybele had just begun,

"Heartwood Hotel, Heartwood Hotel,
Where feathered and furred together can dwell,"

. . . when, "Ahem!"

The door, which they hadn't fully closed, swung open to reveal none other than Mr. Heartwood himself, ducking down to peer into the tiny room. Behind him, Mona could just see Tilly's whiskery face.

"I knew it, sir," said Tilly impatiently. "I knew she was in here."

Mona's heart began to pound. Tilly had told her not to speak with the guests. It was a rule. And she hadn't just been talking with Cybele, she had been sharing secrets and listening to the swallow's singing!

But Mr. Heartwood didn't look the least bit upset. "See, I do. But hear, that, too," replied the badger, who was too big to enter the room but remained, grinning, in the doorway, with Tilly trapped behind him. "Miss Cybele, would you be so kind as to finish your song?"

"I . . . I don't know."

"Please," encouraged Mr. Heartwood.

Cybele paused, then nodded and cleared her throat.

"Heartwood Hotel, Heartwood Hotel,
Where feathered and furred together can dwell,
Where rest can be had from troubles and fears,
Where wings can repair and joy reappears . . ."

It was a happy, warm song of seedcakes and soufflés, bubbly baths and staircases that led up to the stars. It made Mona want to dance. When Cybele was done, not only was Mona clapping, but Mr. Heartwood was, too. Even Tilly reluctantly joined in.

"Brava!" said Mr. Heartwood. "Very well sung, Miss Cybele. I am so sorry to disturb you, but we were looking for our maid"—he gestured to Mona—"and we've found her again. And found something else, too. A voice . . . Yes, what a voice.

Miss Cybele, I know this is a trying time for you, but I must ask, will you share your voice with our guests?"

Cybele gave a small peep, but Mona whispered, "Oh, everyone would love it, and perhaps it would make your stay less lonely."

Cybele paused. Then she slowly nodded. "I guess . . . one song. You've been so generous to me, Mr. Heartwood, it is the least I can do."

"Of course. And if that goes well, and you do choose to keep singing, it would be my honor to waive your room fee in exchange, and upgrade you to a proper bird room as well."

"Really? Are . . . are you sure?" stammered Cybele, hopping off the peg in excitement.

"Sure as my fur." Mr. Heartwood grinned again, his eyes catching sight of the heart just below the peg. He tugged his whiskers as he glanced at Mona and then back at the heart. "I wonder . . ." He gave his whiskers a twirl, then cleared his throat. "Well,

well. Nothing's wrong that ends in song. Miss Tilly had me worried about you, Miss Mona, but no need. Keep up the good work."

"Thank you," said Mona. She couldn't help but smile.

"Humph," said Tilly, but only under her breath. To Mr. Heartwood she said, "I'm glad everything turned out, sir."

Then they all left Cybele's room to return to work. Mona was the last, and when she waved good-bye, she saw that instead of a tear in the swallow's eye, there was a twinkle.

THE WOODPECKER'S WARNING

Cybele's first performance took place at the last dinner of the squirrels' convention. Everyone loved her. She didn't sing just one song—she sang many. Even after the squirrels left, she kept singing every night. Mona was happy to see her grow more confident. It made her feel more confident, too. She had made a friend in Cybele, and in the Sudsburys, who were always requesting her help. But Tilly was still far from friendly. At least to Mona. She did see Tilly bring soup and handkerchiefs to Mrs. Higgins for her cold, and even hot honey to Cybele after a long night of singing. So why did the red squirrel treat Mona differently? She wanted to ask, to know why Tilly behaved the way she did, but they were so busy. There was never time. There was always something going on at the Heartwood Hotel.

RAT-A-TAT-TAT! Mona was in the middle of cleaning Cybele's new room, which was now her job, despite Tilly's protests, when she heard the noise.

RAT-A-TAT-TAT!

The sound came again. Was it a woodpecker? There was a woodpecker, Tony, on staff, but Mona had never properly met him. He was always quick to leave after meals.

She hurried to the shutters and pushed them open, but before she could step out onto the balcony, Tony the woodpecker swooped from a top branch and, spying her,

cried, "Alarm! Alarm! Didn't you hear it? Inside! Inside at once!" Then he clung to the trunk and pounded his beak into it again, *RAT-A-TAT-TAT!*

Mona's heart pounded, too, as she hurried out into the hall, where she ran into Tilly.

The squirrel was frantic. "It's the alarm! Quick, quick, we need to gather in the dining hall."

Mona followed Tilly down the stairs, wondering what could be going on. *Mr. Heartwood will take care of it,* Mona tried to reassure herself.

But in the dining hall, Mr. Heartwood looked as concerned and unsure of what to do as everyone else. Lunch had clearly been interrupted. Plates of food lay half eaten or untouched on the round tables. No one seemed hungry anymore except one shrew, who was gobbling up plateful after plateful in a nervous state.

Most of the staff had gathered on one side of the room, while on the other side the guests huddled, including Cybele and the Sudsburys. The swallow looked frightened, and Lord Sudsbury was sitting on a chair taking deep breaths while Lady Sudsbury rubbed his shoulders. Ms. Prickles was looking after them, offering tea and soothing words. She was clearly upset, too, despite her demeanor, because her quills were raised, and she almost poked a guest!

"I thought this was a safe place," moaned Lord Sudsbury loudly.

"Yes, so did I!" added a chipmunk.

Others joined in the cry, and Mr. Heartwood, hearing this, strode onto the stage. "Please, dear guests, stay calm. There's nothing to fear, as long as the staff of the Heartwood are here. We will keep you safe." Then he gestured to Cybele. "Perhaps some soothing tunes would help calm everyone's nerves."

Cybele took her place onstage again and began to sing, but for once her voice wobbled.

Mr. Heartwood had returned to muttering and

pacing back and forth in front of the staff when the woodpecker swooped in through the doors. He landed next to the badger. The guests looked over questioningly.

"Did everyone hear? Is everyone here?!" the woodpecker said loudly. His crown of red feathers was ruffled and there were wood chips caught in the feathers on his chest.

"Hush!" said Mr. Heartwood. "No need to further alarm anyone. Now tell me at once—quietly—what is going on?" Mr. Heartwood's voice was neither poetic nor poised.

The woodpecker darted his head side to side, at last saying in punctuated but almost whispered words, "It's a bear! A bear, Mr. Heartwood. A great big one. It came right up the path, just as you please!"

"A bear?" Mr. Heartwood exclaimed. "A bear! And what is it doing now, Tony?"

"It's at the front door. Yes. It's at the front door,

trying to get in! It hasn't found the hidden lock, but it could at any moment!"

Maggie and Maurice, the rabbits, threw their paws around each other. Tilly moaned, "Oh, oh, oh," while Mrs. Higgins said sharply, "But it's late fall. Bears should be ready for sleeping." Mr. Heartwood nodded to Mrs. Higgins. "Indeed! What in blithering brambles is he doing here? Tony, your post is the most important of the jobs in this hotel! What were you doing? Were you at rest? You know you cannot! You must protect the guests!"

Mona had never seen Mr. Heartwood so angry at any of the staff before. Tony looked very upset.

"I . . . I . . ." stammered Tony.

But Mr. Heartwood was still furious. He huffed. "Now

see the situation we are in . . . Why, I don't know where to begin!" He tugged his whiskers mightily.

"No respect, no respect whatsoever," said Gilles, and it took Mona a moment to realize he was talking about the bear. "Doesn't he know where he is?"

"We'll have to do something soon," said Mrs. Higgins. "Or Lord Sudsbury . . . Well, you know. . . ." She glanced over at Lord Sudsbury, whose tail was beginning to shake.

"But, Mrs. Higgins, can't we just get rid of him?" cried Tilly. She was trembling, she was so frightened.

"Don't worry, dearie. There, there," Ms. Prickles comforted, having joined them.

She started to say something else to Tilly, but Mona didn't hear, for Maggie, one of the laundry rabbits, burst out, "We can launch an attack from the second-floor windows. We can throw pots and pans—those are heavy. . . ."

"I have shears!" said Mr. Higgins.

"Decorum!" said Mr. Heartwood. "Decorum, everyone! Attack? Do intelligence we lack? We are the Heartwood. We must think of a different plan; we run by rules. We must use these as our . . . as our . . . tools!" His rhyme came in a stammer, which was unlike him.

As the animals clustered and began to discuss, Mona wondered about what Gilles had said about the bear not knowing where he was.

Maybe, thought Mona, *this bear really doesn't know where he is.* Everyone thought he was trying to get into the hotel to attack them, but maybe something else was going on. She remembered the bear's den she had come across during the big storm. It did look a bit like the Heartwood. Could that den be what the bear was looking for?

Mona had to find out quickly, before something bad happened. If the animals attacked him, he would get mad. A mad bear was far different from a bumbling, confused one. She quietly scurried from the crowd.

She had almost reached the dining hall door when Tilly saw her. "Where are you going?" she asked, her eyes wide.

"I . . . I'm going to see the bear. I think he might be lost."

"You're WHAT?" said Tilly. "You have to stay here. Those are the rules. Besides, it's a bear. . . . You can't just . . ."

"But I can," replied Mona. "And I'm going to."

For the first time, Mona ignored Tilly, to Tilly's great annoyance, and headed bravely into the lobby to face the great bear.

BRUMBLE THE BEAR

The lobby was empty and quiet, except for the booming *thump, thump, thump!* coming from the door as the bear pushed his shoulder against it over and over.

Brave as she might have felt before, now that she was alone and facing the thumping, Mona began to tremble.

She took a deep breath to slow her racing heart and marched up to the entrance. When there was a pause in the thumping, she carefully opened the door a crack and slipped out, quickly closing it behind her.

A mountain of black rose up in front of her. The bear was not only gigantic, but also very old. Mona could tell from the silvery streaks in his fur. He smelled like years of fish and dusty dens. He gazed left and right, then back to the Heartwood.

"Shucks. It's just not . . . here," he grumbled. His voice was gravelly and sounded ready for rest.

He seemed confused. Could she be right? Was he lost? Mona had to ask him. She cleared her throat as loudly as she could, trying to get his attention. "Mr. Bear, excuse me."

But the bear didn't hear her. Or even seem to see her. Not even when he pushed on the hotel door with his snout, just missing the heart by inches. Mona jumped out of the way to avoid being crushed. The bear thwacked his nose hard, and the force of it caused him to fall back on his haunches.

"Shucks," he said again in his deep, tired voice.

Mona tried again, a lot louder. "Oh, Mr. Bear!" she shouted. Still no luck.

So she pulled a seedcake left over from breakfast from her apron pocket and threw it up at him. She hadn't expected her aim to be so good. *PLUCK!* It hit him right on his nose.

"Hey." The bear swatted at his nose with his paw, then looked down to see where the cake had come from. He spied Mona.

"I'm sorry," she said.

"Huh?" he replied, blinking at her.

"I'm sorry!" she repeated loudly.

"For what?"

"For the . . ." Mona shook her head. "Oh, never mind." She cleared her throat again. "Mr. Bear," she began.

"Brumble's the name," he said.

"Mr. Brumble, I think you've come to the wrong place."

"Aw, shucks. I wondered why there was a door. I'm looking . . ." He gave a mighty yawn.

"Looking for your winter den?" finished Mona.

"My den?" said the bear, surprised. "It's here?"

"No," said Mona. "This is a hotel."

"Hotel?" Brumble looked up at the giant tree and shook his head in astonishment. "Fancy that."

"I'm afraid we don't have rooms large enough for bears," Mona said. "There is a den," she added, "upstream a ways. Maybe it's yours."

"Ah." Brumble smiled. "That must be it. My memory's just not . . ." He rubbed his nose with his paw and gave another yawn.

"We all forget things," said Mona. "Don't worry."

"Thank you kindly." His eyelids began to droop.

"Do you want to go there?" said Mona.

Brumble's eyes snapped open. "Go where?"

"To your den!"

"Ah. Yes. Of course. Which way did you say it was?"

"Just upstream," said Mona.

"Ah. Good. Better get going, then. There's nothing like home. Just got to find it."

And with that, and another rumbling yawn, Brumble awkwardly pushed himself back up, squishing mushroom lanterns in the process, and turned around and rambled . . . *down*stream!

"Wait!" cried Mona. "You're going the wrong way."

Brumble stopped and shook his head. "Shucks." He gave another yawn and turned around.

What if he got lost again, or fell asleep on the way to his den? Mona made a quick decision. "Mr. Brumble, I can come with you, if you'd like, and show you the way."

"You'd do that?"

Mona nodded.

"Gosh. You sure are nice."

It didn't take long to reach the bear's den. Although at first Mona was very scared, Brumble insisted she ride on his back, and so she did, clinging to his fur and listening to him yawn and ramble. As it turned out, this den wasn't his usual one, and that was part of the reason he was lost. Just as he was beginning his winter sleep, he had been woken up by howling wolves. They were so noisy they kept him up, so he decided to move to his childhood den instead. *Wolves again!* thought Mona. They really *were* in Fernwood Forest.

When they reached the enormous tree, Brumble sighed happily. Mona slid down off his back and watched as he wiggled himself through the opening. It was a tight fit for him now, but she imagined it wouldn't have been when he was a cub.

"If you are ever in need of a Brumble, you'll know where to find me," he said to her from inside the den, his voice muffled. His black tail disappeared into the darkness. "Home," he said. "There's nowhere like home." And then came a yawn—and snoring.

Brumble's words echoed in Mona's mind as she hurried back to the Heartwood.

By the time Mona returned, slipping under blackberry vines and in through the garden door, the hotel seemed to be back to normal. No alarms or terrified guests, only the sound of Cybele's sweet voice drifting from the ballroom. She headed downstairs, hoping to find Mr. Heartwood. She wanted to tell him what Brumble had said about the wolves. Instead, she found Tilly in the kitchen, poking her paw into an acorn soufflé. Tilly's tail was bristled up and her paws seemed to be shaking.

The squirrel looked up at Mona, gulped down her bite, and snapped, "Where have YOU been? Were you hiding? Well, it's about time you came back. We have to get the dining hall ready. Mr.

Heartwood is throwing a special dinner for the guests to make up for this morning. The bear is gone."

"I know," said Mona proudly. "I wasn't hiding. I was the one who took him home. And he told me something, too. . . . I need to talk to Mr. Heartwood."

Tilly's eyes grew wide. Then they narrowed. "I wouldn't talk to Mr. Heartwood if I were you. You shouldn't have left your post. That's a rule."

"But I was helping the bear," said Mona.

"And now you need to help me," said Tilly. "Come on. We have work to do."

Mona hesitated. But Brumble had moved closer to the Heartwood to get away from the wolves, so that meant they were still a long way away. Too far from the hotel to cause trouble.

At least, that's what she hoped.

THE FRONT-DESK DISASTER

The incident with the bear had left a feeling of unease among the guests. Mr. Heartwood ordered that no staff were to mention the occurrence. And so Mona kept thoughts of Brumble to herself over the next few weeks, while she worked extra hard to prepare for the First Snow Festival.

Everyone was working hard. Ms. Prickles was already planning out the dishes, including lots of hearty soups and stews and ginger cakes. Cybele was practicing new songs, good ones to dance to, and Mr. Higgins had stacked wood by the hearth, ready for the first fire. Mona had spent hours helping Tilly clean out the walnut-shell lanterns and putting new candles inside each one. On the day of the festival, they all—guests and staff—would get to decorate the outside of the tree with the lanterns, hanging them off the branches from the balconies. And then they would light them, just for the night, to welcome the First Snow.

It was, according even to Tilly, beautiful.

Will I get to see it? Mona wondered. Mr. Heartwood hadn't mentioned her leaving—not even when he gave her her first Fernwood farthings—nor had Mrs. Higgins, but Tilly was always reminding her.

When Mona asked her if she could put up a pretty black-and-white picture that Lady Sudsbury wanted to give her in their room, Tilly said, "You can't take gifts from guests! That's a rule. And there's no point in decorating anyway. You won't be here much longer."

Mona knew Tilly was right. After all, the fall

season ended with the First Snow Festival. And she was only supposed to stay for the fall.

The air grew crisper, more guests arrived, more decorations were hung, and soon the festival was only a day away. It had been a busy morning, and as Mona was passing through the lobby on her way to lunch, Gilles asked her to watch the front desk.

"I've just had word from the messenger jay. The Newtons have cancelled," he cried, with a tsk and a flick of his tongue. "This will never do. I must tell Mr. Heartwood. Those newts are some of our oldest guests, and they *always* book the penthouse for the First Snow. Now the suite will sit empty! This is almost worse than a bad review in the *Pinecone Press*. Now, a *good* review . . . well, that just might change things."

It wasn't the first time Mona had watched the desk. She often did when Gilles took sun-basking breaks on sunny days.

"You remember where the papers are? Not that anyone is likely to come in, mind. There are no expected check-ins."

"Yes," said Mona, straightening her apron.

Gilles set a stack of books on the chair, and Mona climbed up them and settled on top. When the lizard left, she sighed and gazed over at the hearth. The leaf garlands had long been taken down, and now a string of tiny holly berries hung across it. She was imagining the hearth all crackling and cozy when her thoughts were interrupted by a small voice, "Excuse me, a little service please?"

Mona looked across the desk but saw no one. She stood up on the piles of books and peered over the desk. A large June bug stared back up at her, antennas twitching. She was shiny emerald-purple, like an iridescent jewel, and was wearing glittering dark glasses. Four of the bug's six legs were holding tiny suitcases.

"Oh, hello," said Mona as politely as she could. She clambered down from the books and hurried around the desk.

The bug set down her suitcases. "I must say, it certainly wasn't easy to find this establishment," she huffed.

"Oh," said Mona. "I'm so sorry to hear that."

"There were no maps, no directions. Not even a sign," the bug went on. "But I suppose security is the purpose?" The bug paused and surveyed the lobby.

"Of course," agreed Mona, adding, "How can I help you?"

"Most obviously I am seeking accommodation," said the bug. "I am looking for a room. The most commendable room you can offer. I have come to stay for your festival."

"It is a wonderful festival," said Mona enthusiastically. "If you could just wait a moment for our front-desk staff—"

"Are *you* not at the front desk?" The June bug twitched her antennas in displeasure.

"Yes, well, of course," said Mona. She thought for a moment. "We do have the penthouse suite available, and it *is* our grandest room."

"Grand, hmm." The bug looked a little surprised. "That seems satisfactory."

"Could I have your name?"

The bug paused, "Ms. J, if you please."

"Your full name?" asked Mona.

The insect paused again. "That is my full name," she replied decisively.

"Oh, okay. Well, Ms. J, I assure you we can make the room fit your needs." Mona smiled. "Extra pillows for the bed, and stools and stepladders— so it's easy to reach things."

"Ah," Ms. J said, seeming surprised again. "Yes, that should be adequate." She opened one of her four suitcases, which was full of Fernwood farthings.

"It will be five, please," said Mona, checking

the room-fee form to make sure. It was only one farthing for a regular room, but the penthouse was extra expensive, of course.

Ms. J handed the farthings to Mona, one by one. Then she opened another case and took out a notebook and pen.

As Ms. J jotted something down, Mona climbed up to the desk to prepare the check-in form. She couldn't believe she was booking the penthouse! And just after Gilles had been so unhappy about the cancellation. He would be really pleased. Maybe he would even tell Mr. Heartwood.

"Here is your key," said Mona, scampering back down and around the desk to hand it to the bug. The key was almost as big as Ms. J. But the bug didn't seem to mind. It was on a string, which she looped through the handle of one of her suitcases.

"The penthouse is on the top floor," said Mona. "The dining hall is open all day. There is a games room and a salon on the second floor. Tomorrow is the big festival. The lantern lighting will take place at dusk and will be followed by a big feast."

"Yes, yes," said the June bug. "And what of your precautions against predators? There was rumor of a bear?"

Mona gulped. She knew Mr. Heartwood didn't want anyone talking about it, but she thought the truth was probably best. "That was a simple misunderstanding on the part of Brumb—of the bear. We all work together here at Heartwood to provide you with the utmost comfort and safety. See?"—Mona pointed at the sign above the hearth—"We Live by 'Protect and Respect,' Not by 'Tooth and Claw.'"

"Hmm, I shall see about that," said Ms. J, jotting something else in her notebook. "I would prefer a statement that refers specifically to no prejudice against six-legged creatures. But you assure me that there will be no complications during my stay? I've heard of a policy. . . ."

Mona paused. Hadn't Tilly once said something

about six-leggeds and needing to be extra careful since they were so small? Surely that wouldn't be a problem. "Everything will be fine," she said.

The bug looked at her with her antennas twitching, as though wanting more.

"I . . . I promise," she added.

"Very well," the bug finally said. "The top floor, you say?"

"Yes, to the right. Do you need help with your bags? Or the key?"

The June bug declined and put away her notebook. Then she picked up her suitcases and, to Mona's surprise, began to fly. Weighted by her suitcases and the key, the bug was a little wobbly, but she soon disappeared up the stairs with the key dangling down.

Mona watched proudly, then made a note to send up pillows and stepladders.

"Is that a bug I see heading upstairs?" cried Gilles, arriving back at the desk a second later.

"Yes," said Mona. "Her name is Ms. J. She's just booked the penthouse."

"An insect?" cried Gilles. "You booked an insect?" Gilles's tongue flashed in and out furiously. "Don't you know anything? There are NO bugs at the Heartwood."

And that's when Mona remembered that Tilly had never actually said what the rule was about six-leggeds. Mona had just assumed the rule was to be extra careful not to step on them—not that bugs weren't allowed in the hotel at all! Then immediately she remembered Ms. J's concern regarding complications. Had Ms. J known what the rule was about? "But . . . I don't understand. I . . . I told her that there would be no problem. I . . . I promised."

"You PROMISED? That does it!" cried Gilles. "We can't ask her to leave. That would cause too much of a fuss. Oh . . . Mr. Heartwood is going to be furious."

"B-but . . ." stammered Mona. She still didn't

understand. "Should I do anything . . . ?"

"You've done enough already," said Gilles, shaking his head and sighing deeply. "Just go."

Mona stumbled away from the desk toward the stairs, not knowing where exactly she *should* go. Maybe the kitchen. Maybe Ms. Prickles would make her feel better.

But in the kitchen, instead of Ms. Prickles, she found Tilly, munching some nuts.

"What's the matter with you?" said Tilly.

Mona told her, in halting words. Tilly's eyes flashed.

"You broke *another* rule!"

"I was only trying to help, to treat a guest with respect, like the sign says. . . ."

"Help?! You're going to be in heaps of trouble! Heaps!"

"But—"

"You'll be fired for sure." Tilly smirked. "If I were you, I'd leave now."

Tears pricked Mona's eyes as Tilly kept going. But Mona wasn't listening anymore. She was trying not to cry. She didn't want to. Not in front of Tilly. She never thought she would be fired. She thought she had been doing the right thing. But Gilles was so upset. Tilly was probably right. Mr. Heartwood was nice, but he did have his rules and he could get really mad. She remembered how he was when Brumble had been there not so long ago.

But she was mad, too. Mad at Tilly! Maybe if Tilly hadn't always been so short with her, she would know the rules and the reasons for them!

"I know you've never liked me," she burst, "though I don't know why. I've always tried to do my best. We could have been friends. But you don't want any friends. Ms. Prickles said you have hurts, but all I think is that you like hurting others! You're always trying to get me in trouble. Well, I hope you're happy, because now you have!"

Tilly was speechless.

Mona didn't wait for Tilly to respond. She took off her apron and threw it down, hard, on the kitchen table. Her mind was a rush of emotions, and her paws rushed, too—downstairs.

Mona had to leave anyway. Why not now? Before Mr. Heartwood fired her.

And so, whiskers trembling, she put the far-things she'd earned in her pocket and collected her suitcase. Clutching it tightly, she returned to the kitchen—Tilly was thankfully no longer there— and stuffed the case full of seedcakes and a jar of honey. Then, though her heart told her not to, Mona the mouse left the Heartwood Hotel.

THE WICKED WOLVES

Fernwood Forest had changed in the months Mona had been at the Heartwood, even since her adventure with Brumble. Except for the evergreens, the trees were now mostly bare, and the ground was cold and hard on Mona's paws. Plants and flowers had tucked themselves away, and the stream was flowing slowly, gurgling, *Winter's near. It's almost here. Winter's near. . . .*

Yes, the forest had changed, but Mona had changed, too. Before, she hadn't minded the slumbering, slow forest, as long as she had some food and a place to sleep. Now it felt so lonely and cold and quiet. Already she missed the warm mossy carpets and the chatter of the guests, the smell of the seedcakes and the song of the swallow. She missed the hotel.

But she couldn't go back. Not only because of the rules (which, truthfully, she didn't regret breaking) or how she'd left, rushing out (which already she *did* regret) but because she wasn't wanted. Tilly had made that clear.

And so Mona trudged on, looking for somewhere she could sleep. The daylight was fading and she tried not to think too much about the First Snow Festival and all the excitement she'd be missing.

When night arrived, she found a hollow log and clambered inside. The log was damp—too damp to make a good home—but mostly protected from the wind. Mona curled up beside her suitcase and traced the heart with one paw. Her stomach rumbled and she took out one of the seedcakes—only one, because she wanted them to last.

As she nibbled it, the taste brought back a memory—the smell of toasted seedcakes with acorn butter, and her mother's voice, "Seedcakes for my sweet Mona." The picture in her mind was fuzzy, but now she was certain, her mom *had* made seedcakes for her. Seedcakes that tasted exactly like this. But how had she gotten Ms. Prickles's recipe? Now Mona would never know. She had ruined her chances of finding out. Her appetite disappeared and she couldn't finish the seedcake. She put it back, touching the heart once more as she closed the case. She shivered. If only she had a cup of Ms. Prickles's hot honey tea. She was just closing her eyes to dream of one when she heard a voice.

"Anytime now, I reckon. And then we feast. Scrumptious squirrels, heavenly hares, meaty moles!"

The voice sent shivers up and down Mona's spine.

"Ah, shut your trap," came another voice. "You're making me drool."

"Me too."

"Me three."

And then a whole chorus of them chimed in, yessing and yipping and pawing the ground. It was wolves! Mona clutched her case tight and kept very, very still.

When the yipping ended, one particularly gruff-sounding wolf said, "The plan had better work."

"Of course it's going to work. We wait till we see the lit-up tree. The tree with lights, that's the one. More than enough animals in there to feed our pack and then some."

But the gruff wolf continued, "Something's going to go wrong. I just know it. I don't like all this waiting, Gnarl."

"Waiting is better than chasing jackrabbits, Wince. Did I tell you 'bout the time I found that mole clubhouse? Ah, I wasn't hungry for a week, I say."

"How can we forget, with you wearing that badge around your neck like you're . . . you're too good for us."

"So what if I do, Wince? What's so bad about being a little more refined?"

"We don't need all that fancy stuff. We just need our noses and our teeth. Besides, it's just a myth, this 'hotel.' And we could've been hunting now, instead of meeting and planning and waiting."

"Well, if you're so eager, Wince, then why don't you just go back to the Great Woods? It'll leave more for us, more for me."

"You're sure you're right about the lights?"

"I told you, yes. I've heard rumors about the Heartwood. Lots of rumors. I'm right about the lights. They're supposed to be lit when the snow falls. It's getting colder. Should be soon. And when they're lit, we'll find it. It's around here somewhere. The Heartwood Hotel."

"Heartwood—mmm. I like the hearts. They're tastiest," broke in another wolf.

"You're too bad," said another. "A big bad wolf." And the wolves began to howl again with laughter.

Mona trembled all over. Slowly, carefully, she peeked out through a hollow knot in the log.

It was a whole pack of them. Some pacing, some lying down, licking their paws. Moonlight glanced off sharp teeth and eyes yellow like fire. She could see the one—Gnarl—who was wearing the moles' badge. It was hanging around his neck from a ribbon that was tattered and maybe even a little bloody. Mona crouched back down in the hollow log, her heart beating so fast it was a hum. That's why wolves had been roaming nearby for months. They'd been searching for the Heartwood

Hotel, waiting for the lights to be put up! She had to do something.

But before she could do anything, one of the wolves, the one called Wince, barked, "Hey! Shut it! I smell something!"

Mona froze.

"Ah, you're crazy."

"No! I smell something." The sound of sniffing filled the air. "Mouse meat! I'm sure of it!"

Mona dared not move. Even her tail was as motionless as a twig.

She heard the padding of the wolves' paws as a few more got up to join Wince. The sound of their footsteps came closer . . . and closer.

This was it. In a moment they would find her and gobble her up, and there would be no one to warn Mr. Heartwood and the others about their terrible plan.

And then, just when she was sure it was all over . . .

"Give it up, Wince. You're just imagining things. All the tasty treats are in the hotel."

"But—" grumbled Wince.

"I tell you! All the animals are there. That's where they all go this time of year. And that's where we'll find them."

"Fine, Gnarl," muttered Wince, and Mona could hear him lie down with a thump. "I guess even my nose is hungry."

"We're all hungry," replied Gnarl. "But soon we won't be. Soon the Heartwood will be ours. But not tonight. I'm going to get some shut-eye. I suggest you get some sleep, too—rest your stomach before the big feast."

Again the pack agreed. It wasn't long before the yeses and yips turned to grunts and snores, and Mona felt her heart begin to slow again.

But it was only after the wolves were completely quiet that she took another peek. They were asleep, a mass of gray and black. Carefully, she tiptoed out of the hollow log and crept around them, barely daring to breathe. They were so close she could smell their vile breath and see the drool dripping from their fangs.

Once she had passed the last one, she began to run, faster than she ever had before, toward the Heartwood.

TILLY TELLS THE TRUTH

Mona had never scurried so quickly. She followed the stream this way and that, all the way back up to the hotel. The moonlight glimmered off the water, showing her the way.

She reached the tree, with its huge canopy of branches and the tiny carved heart, just as the sun was beginning to awaken, stretching its rays across the forest. Mona didn't hesitate. She opened the door and dashed inside.

There was no one in the lobby. *The guests must still be sleeping,* thought Mona. But the staff would already be up, eating their breakfast. And so she scampered down the stairs and burst into the kitchen, where, as she expected, the staff were all gathered around the kitchen table.

"I saw wolves!" cried Mona.

Everyone stared. Tilly stopped fidgeting with her food, her mouth open in surprise. Mr. Heartwood looked at Mona stonily. But Ms. Prickles smiled and said, "You're back, dearie!"

"Now, where in the forest did you—" started Mrs. Higgins.

"Hush now, at once," said Mr. Heartwood. "Miss Mona, please go to my office, or take a seat. Your stories must wait; first we eat."

"But, Mr. Heartwood . . . Mrs. Higgins . . . Ms. Prickles . . . you have to listen. I saw wolves! A whole pack of them."

"Hush, I say!" Mr. Heartwood was looking more and more agitated. "The hotel hasn't been found by wolves yet. Why would they now be a threat? The wolves don't even frequent Fernwood Forest."

"But . . . but they have been seen nearby," stammered Gilles. "I heard a guest discussing—"

"Enough!" bellowed Mr. Heartwood.

"But you have to believe me," cried Mona. "If this is about Ms. J, I thought we welcomed all guests here."

"As we should," said Mr. Heartwood, his tone suddenly softening, "and from now on we will. I was concerned small guests might be in danger from large paws, but instead of taking the time to make proper accommodations, I was a fool and made a rule. That must change. No excuses." After a pause, he continued, more sternly now, "But there's another matter here, Miss Mouse. By leaving without speaking to me, you broke my trust and your pledge."

"I . . . I . . ." stammered Mona, trying to explain. But the explanation came from Tilly.

"It wasn't her fault!" cried Tilly, leaping up and

knocking over a bowl of honey. "It was mine."

Everyone froze, even Mona. Tilly's tail twitched behind her head. "It was my fault Mona left. I tricked her. I said she had to, that she would be fired."

"You did?" humphed the badger. "Please explain."

"Indeed," said Mrs. Higgins, rubbing her nose furiously.

"I'm sorry. I thought that sooner or later you would choose her over me." Tilly gulped. "Mona was doing so well. She soothed the skunks and the swallow and rescued us from the bear. . . ."

"You did, dearie?" Ms. Prickles looked over at Mona, impressed.

Mona nodded, blushing.

Tilly continued, "She did. She talked the bear into leaving. I knew but didn't say. She's a good maid. A better one than me. And if she says there are wolves, then we should believe her."

Tilly's speech left the room silent, except for the *plop, plop, plop* of the honey spilling over the edge of the table. Mona couldn't believe it. She tried to catch Tilly's eye, but the squirrel didn't meet her gaze.

At last Mr. Heartwood spoke, but it wasn't to Mona or to Tilly. It was up to the ceiling, as though he was speaking to the hotel itself. "So the wolves have found us at last."

"No, they haven't," piped Mona. "Not yet. But they will. They know about our lights. They are watching the forest to see which tree gets lit up. Then they will come. Unless we do something."

"But what, dearie?" said Ms. Prickles, whose quills were flared out, though her voice remained calm as always. "What can we possibly do?"

Mona had no idea. But Mr. Heartwood did.

"With no lit tree, there's nothing for them to see," he declared. "We simply don't put up the lanterns."

"But what about the party? The lighting of the hearth?" said Mrs. Higgins. "All this work . . . The guests are expecting—"

"No fire," said Mr. Heartwood with a worried look. "The smoke will rise and catch the wolves' eyes."

"What about the food?" said Ms. Prickles. "My ginger cakes? My acorn soufflé?"

Mr. Heartwood looked increasingly troubled. "No feast either, I fear," he said, shaking his head. "The delicious smells might draw the wolves near."

"So . . . no festival, then, Mr. Heartwood?" said Mrs. Higgins, her nose redder than ever. "First the summer festivals, and now . . ."

Mr. Higgins placed a comforting paw on hers, and she almost smiled.

But then Mr. Heartwood said, "No festival. This is serious. Hurry, before they wake. Place notes under the doors of all the guests, informing them at once of the change of plans."

The Heartwood ♡ Hotel

Dear Guest,

We regret to inform you that the First Snow Festival has been cancelled. There will be a meeting in the ballroom this morning for any questions.

—The Heartwood Management

The Heartwood Hoax

Even before breakfast was served, the ballroom was bustling with guests, notes in paws and claws.

The staff gathered near the stage, while the guests, many still in their nightcaps and gowns, crowded in the middle of the room. Ms. J was standing on a table with her book, asking another guest, a chatty chipmunk, some pointed questions. Cybele was comforting an admiring shrew, who was very disappointed the swallow would not be singing that night. Lord Sudsbury was pacing, his tail trembling, with Lady Sudsbury, whose fur was in curlers, by his side. "There, there, my

sweet," she said. "There's nothing to fret about."

But Mona knew differently. It seemed strange to see the ballroom so colorfully decorated, with holly berries and spiderweb snowflakes hanging from the ceiling and the tables draped in leaf-skeleton lace, when tonight's celebrations had been cancelled.

Mr. Heartwood strode onto the stage under a banner that read FIRST SNOW FESTIVAL. He straightened his tie and cleared his throat. "Good morning," he said. "As you know, there has been a

change of plans. Unfortunately, due to unforeseen circumstances, we must delay this festive day."

Everyone started asking questions at once.

"But why?" said the chipmunk.

"That's why I came here!" complained the shrew. "I was planning to dance till my paws hurt!"

"And the decorating!" added a small rabbit.

"Yes, explain yourself, Mr. Heartwood!" demanded Lady Sudsbury.

Mr. Heartwood tugged at his robe. "The reasons are . . . complicated. But you will be compensated.

This I promise. And there will be complimentary hot honey and acorn cookies tonight, and Heartwood Hotel cards to play with."

"Cards and cookies!" cried the chipmunk. "That's crumbs! I'm heading home."

"Me too! No festival means no fun," said the shrew.

"No! You must stay!" exclaimed Mr. Heartwood. "It isn't safe."

"Not safe?" screeched the shrew. "What do you mean?"

"I knew it, I knew it!" cried Lord Sudsbury, his tail atremble. "We're under attack! It's the wolves! They're here at last."

The guests gasped.

"They're not here!" said Mr. Heartwood, trying to calm everyone down. "But they are . . . well, near."

That was the wrong thing to say. Now all the guests were panicking. Lord Sudsbury's tail began to shake violently. Cybele looked frightened. "I still can't fly properly!" she moaned. Ms. J was pacing on top of a table, writing furiously.

"You must stay here!" said Mr. Heartwood. "We all must hide."

"No! We have to run away!" cried a guest.

Others joined in with their suggestions. Mona listened from her spot by the stage, her ears twitching. Running or hiding: those were the choices. Running or hiding: that's what small animals like her did. That's what she had done all her life. She had run away from the Heartwood because she was afraid she had made a mistake. But she was happy she had let in the June bug, and proud of helping the Sudsburys and making friends with Cybele. She was especially proud of helping Brumble. She didn't want to run anymore, or hide either. She didn't want the wolves to ruin everything. She wanted to have the festival. She wanted to decorate the tree. . . .

And just as she thought that, she had an idea! A

way to decorate a tree *and* get rid of the wolves. It was time to take Brumble up on his offer.

"It's time that we made the *wolves* run and hide, for a change!" cried Mona, excited.

Mona didn't realize she had said it aloud. But she had. And loudly, too. Loudly enough that it cut through the other conversations and the animals turned to her. "The wolves?" "What do you mean?" "You've got to be kidding!" But then Cybele said strongly in her sweet voice, "Wait! I want to hear. What is it, Mona? What is your plan?"

And so Mona explained. And as she explained, the eyes of the animals grew wide and bright with the power of a big idea, of a brave idea, of a brilliant idea.

Fernwood Forest was dark when the animals made their way upstream. Of course, many of the guests stayed safely in the hotel (Mr. Sudsbury hid in his room), but quite a few did join in. Which was good, since it took the work of many paws and claws and wings to lift the lanterns upstream to the big hollow tree where Brumble slept. The animals barely spoke, just scurried, swift and silent as only small animals can be. They brought peppermint, too—in big bundles—to line Brumble's tree and mask his scent, another part of Mona's plan.

It was cold and blustery and the air smelled like snow. Mona held tight to her unlit lantern, which swung wildly back and forth. When the howls of the wolves were carried by the wind, the animals all paused, and only when the sound faded did they start again.

When they reached the big tree, they stopped. The sound of snoring rumbled from inside.

"I'll wake him," said Mona. "I know Brumble."

No one, not even Mr. Heartwood, argued.

Mona set down her lantern and scurried through the opening, into the darkness and the smell of fur and fish and berries. Quickly, her eyes adjusted

and she realized she was standing right in front of Brumble's nose!

She gulped.

Brumble was a lot bigger than she had remembered.

It was one thing to imagine the plan—imagine Brumble happily agreeing. But would he really be so happy to be woken from his sleep? Mona wasn't sure.

She gulped again. She could turn back, run away, hide. . . . But she didn't.

And so she said, in her biggest voice, "BRUMBLE! WAKE UP!"

Brumble's ear twitched but his eyes did not open.

"BRUMBLE, WAKE UP!" she tried again.

Brumble's other ear twitched. He snorted. But still he snored on.

Mona reached into her apron pocket and pulled out a piece of honeycomb wrapped in a leaf. She

had brought it just in case. It was very sticky. "BRUMBLE, PLEASE, IT'S MONA!" she cried for the third time, in her very loudest voice, and held up the honeycomb.

The bear's nose wiggled. His tongue stuck out and, with a big lick, he gobbled up the honeycomb, covering Mona's paw in drool.

"Mmmm, good," he mumbled, his eyes flickering open. He gave a huge yawn. Mona tumbled backward from the force of it.

Brumble looked at her sleepily and said, "Gosh! It's you. . . ."

"I—I'm so sorry to disturb you, Brumble," stammered Mona, "but I need your help."

It took Mona a few tries to explain the idea, because Brumble kept falling back asleep, but when he finally heard and understood it all, he liked it well enough. "Those noisy wolves are the reason I had to move my home in the first place," he grumbled.

And Brumble especially liked Mr. Heartwood's offer of more honeycomb and berries as well, to be ready for him upon spring awakening.

And so, Mona went back out and told everyone Brumble was in agreement. The first part of the plan had worked. The next, lining the tree with peppermint, was easy enough, too. But putting up the lanterns proved much more difficult. The wind blustered, and it made balancing on the branches with the lanterns very difficult.

The walnut shells were too big for Mona to hang up herself, so, while the squirrels and chipmunks and birds hooked the lanterns onto the branches, she took the most dangerous job— lighting them. When they were all up and ready, Mona scrambled back and forth, balancing oh-so-carefully on the limbs, and lit each candle. The flames flickered in the wind but miraculously stayed lit.

Soon there were only a few more candles to light. But Mona wanted to get every last one. The candles were small and would burn down quickly. If the wolves didn't see the lights, if the trick didn't work, it would be her fault. And so she stayed, lighting lantern after lantern until the very last one was ablaze.

When she was finished, she blew out her candle, climbed down to join the others, and looked up. The tree was beautiful, as though it were hung with stars. For a second Mona didn't feel like a tiny mouse at all, but big as a bear. Maybe even as big as a tree.

"It's not the Heartwood, but it just might do," said Mr. Heartwood with a nod. "As long as the wolves think so, too."

Just as he said the words: *AWOOO!* The howls made Mona jump.

"Come, quickly!" commanded Mr. Heartwood. The few animals remaining obeyed at once, scurrying away from the tree, into the bushes, out of sight.

AWOOO! The howls grew louder, closer.

"Stop!" commanded Mr. Heartwood. "We'll make too much noise if we move."

It was true, but what would they do? They had no peppermint left to disguise their scent.

"As long as the wolves head to the tree, we shall be safe," said the badger. "As long as the plan works. . . ."

Would it? Mona hoped so with all her heart. She could hear the wolves even louder now. . . .

AWOOOO!

Mona peered out between the branches of the bush. She couldn't see the wolves yet, but she could see Brumble's tree glittering in the darkness.

All at once, she froze. Not just the tree was glittering. The forest was, too—with eyes. The yellow eyes of the wolves.

Any moment now they would find the tree. Any moment they would see the lanterns, too.

And then something terrible happened.

WHOOSH!

A great gust of wind tore through the forest, so strong it whipped back branches, snapped away twigs, and, with a mighty *WHISH*, blew out the lanterns.

Being Brave

"Oh no," whispered Mona. She turned with wide eyes to Mr. Heartwood, who looked horrified, too.

Tilly was shaking, twisting her tail this way and that. "What will we do? What will we do?" she repeated.

Mona gazed back at the tree. All the lanterns were out—at least on the left. But maybe some were still lit on the other side. She had no chance to find out, for at that very moment, the wolves slunk into the clearing.

"I thought I saw something," said one. It was the wolf wearing the badge around his neck—Gnarl.

He looked up, at the dark side of the tree, and shook his head.

"Well, you didn't," said another. "It was just your imagination." He growled in frustration. "And now you're making me imagine things, too. I swear I can smell 'em!"

Another wolf sniffed.

"I can, too! I can, too! Over there." The wolf pointed with his nose in the very direction of the bushes where they were hidden. He sniffed deeply.

"This isn't imagination. I smell meat! I smell fur! I smell food!"

Mona's heart raced. Mr. Heartwood and Tilly were pressed up against her. She could feel Mr. Heartwood trembling and the pounding of Tilly's heart.

The sound of sniffing filled the air. Any second now, the wolves would find them.

The wind was only a whisper now, but strong enough to carry their scent to the wolves' noses. Strong enough to sway the branches of the big tree . . . and reveal a flicker of light. A lantern! It had to be! The lanterns *were* still lit on the other side of the tree. But the wolves would never see them now, not unless Mona did something.

And so she did.

She burst out of the bushes, before Tilly or Mr. Heartwood could stop her.

The wolves saw her at once.

"HEY!" cried one. "That meat is mine!"

"No, it's mine!" cried another.

Mona scurried faster than she ever had before, as fast as a jackrabbit. The wolves were right behind her. She hopped over the roots, tumbled over a fallen twig, regained her footing, and ran to the other side of Brumble's tree.

The lanterns were still lit on this side—but Mona did not stop to admire them. Not at all. She flung herself into the opening, landing with a thud against the bear's great furry side. She had made it! Her breathing was sharp and quick, and her heart was pounding.

Brumble's eyes flickered open. He had fallen asleep again! "Mona . . ." he started.

"Hush," said Mona. "The wolves," she whispered, gesturing to the opening.

"Ah," said Brumble, nodding knowingly. And they both pricked their ears to hear. . . .

"The lights are here! It *is* the tree!" said one of the wolves.

"Isn't as fancy as I figured," said another. "It isn't as big as I thought either."

"Big enough, Wince. Stop your complaining. No wonder we smelled all those tasty treats. We're here! We found it! The Heartwood at last."

"Hush, hush. Not too loud now, or we'll alert them. We've got to be sneaky."

"What're you? Stupid? That mouse'll alert them right away! Come on!"

"I can't smell any animals, only . . . peppermint," griped Wince.

"Minty meat, yum!" said another.

"Forget it. It's the lights that matter."

"Yeah," said another. "And look—the door is open! Come on, you and me, Wince. We'll go first."

Mona pressed herself against the side of the tree, holding her breath, peering through a small knothole, watching as the two wolves began to creep their way in. Brumble's fur bristled, and then . . .

"ROAR!"

Brumble's growl shook the tree from top to bottom.

"YIP, YIP, YIP!" cried the two wolves as they flew backward, tumbling over each other. Their eyes were wide with fright.

"What is it? What's going on?" cried the others.

But the two wolves had no time to respond, for out came Brumble: no longer slow or bumbling but huge and ferocious, standing on his hind legs and roaring. The wolves cowered.

Brumble growled and swatted at the air. The pack of wolves, too stunned to fight back, whimpered, turned tail, and . . . fled.

Fled into the forest. Fled across the stream. Fled and were gone, into the darkness.

Brumble snorted and dropped down to all fours. With a satisfied grunt, he lumbered back into his den. He gave a big yawn.

"Ha! That should teach 'em."

"Thank you," said Mona. "I promise I won't bother you again."

But Brumble didn't respond. He was already asleep.

Mona smiled—and suddenly felt very tired herself. Tired, but happy. The plan—her plan—had worked.

A True Home

All night long the party raged at the *real* Heartwood Hotel. Honey flowed, salted acorns steamed, and the hearth glowed with a crackling fire. Mr. Heartwood sent Tony to check and make sure the wolves were really gone before he lit it, and they were. But even so, the animals were extra careful about the smoke; two crows sat on watch above the chimney, fanning it away.

Those who were there and had seen the wolves flee described the spectacle over and over, but the story never grew old. Some even wrote about it in the guest book. The lanterns had done their job.

They would have to collect them later, but not right now. Right now it was time to celebrate.

Cybele sang. Ms. Prickles danced. Mr. Higgins and Mrs. Higgins were sharing seedcakes. At last Mrs. Higgins seemed to be over her cold, though she still seemed tired—ready for hibernation, perhaps, and a true rest. Mona spied Tilly near the buffet and went over to talk. She wanted to find out exactly why the squirrel had stuck up for her at breakfast.

But before she had a chance, Mr. Heartwood took her aside. "Miss Mona, if you please."

"What is it, Mr. Heartwood?" she asked.

His eyes crinkled. "The heart and spirit you showed today—now I know. It's the same spirit I saw in a mouse pair long ago."

"What do you mean?" Mona's heart began to race.

Mr. Heartwood's eyes were soft. "It was long ago, when the hotel was simply known as the Fernwood. Few frequented our doors, and I was beginning to doubt whether we could make a go of it. There was a storm, much like the one that you arrived in. Two mice knocked on the hotel door. They were drenched and had no money. All they had was a suitcase with a heart on it. I took them in and let them stay in a small room, the same one that Cybele stayed in when she first came here. Mrs. Madeline loved Ms. Prickles's seedcakes, and Mr. Timothy was quite the carver. Through the wind and the snow, they stayed. When spring came and it was time to go, they were so thankful, so full of heart, that Mr. Timothy carved—"

"The heart in the room? And the one on the door?" burst Mona.

"Yes," said Mr. Heartwood. "Yes, indeed."

"You think . . . you think they were my parents? Madeline and Timothy?"

"Of that, I can't be sure. But I have a feeling, in the heart right here." He patted his chest. "It was they who convinced me to change the name. I was reluctant to name it after myself, but they insisted I should, that it was a way to show everyone there is true heart in the Heartwood."

Mona gasped. She was so proud. Not only had her parents stayed there—they had helped give the hotel its name! She couldn't help herself. She threw her arms around the badger in a hug.

"There, there, little one," he said, patting her head. "That was just for you. But the next piece of news, for you as well, I'd like the whole house to hear me tell." Mr. Heartwood took the stage, with Mrs. Higgins beside him, as Mona's thoughts swirled.

So her family *had* stayed at the Heartwood . . . and her suitcase . . . the heart on it—it was the very same heart as the ones here. But just as she had that thought, she remembered: her suitcase . . . She had lost her suitcase. She must have dropped it on her rush back.

Her thoughts were broken by Mr. Heartwood's voice. "I have an announcement to make," he declared, straightening his tie. "Miss Mona, would you please step forth?"

Mona didn't know what was going on. She looked at Tilly, but Tilly shrugged. Clearly she didn't know either.

Even after all the fear and excitement of the day, and the news of her family, Mona's heart quickened as she walked up on the stage.

"Mrs. Higgins, if you please," said Mr. Heartwood.

And from her pocket, Mrs. Higgins produced none other than a Heartwood Hotel key. The hedgehog passed it to the badger, who placed it around Mona's neck with a big, toothless grin. His voice was gruff but choked with emotion as he said, "Mona the mouse, this key is for you. You're one of the Heartwood, loyal and true."

The key was made of wood, with a heart-shaped top. Like the heart on her suitcase. She'd had that suitcase for as long as she could remember. But as she touched the key around her neck and everyone clapped and cheered, she realized she didn't need it anymore.

After all, she wasn't going anywhere. Maybe someone else would find it. Maybe it would take them somewhere special, like it had taken her. The more she thought about it, the more she was certain—the heart on her suitcase had been a sign. Especially if her parents had stayed here, too. *Home* is *where the heart is,* thought Mona. And the Heartwood Hotel was a very fine home, indeed.

And then, when the clapping and cheering began to fade, Ms. J, who was standing on a table with a tiny cup of honey, raised her glass and said, "Well, this is a first. I didn't think so at the beginning, but after this, I must say, this hotel will be getting a five-acorn review in the *Pinecone Press.*"

Now that caused a kerfuffle! Ms. J was the reviewer for the *Pinecone Press*! Mr. Heartwood was astounded. *Everyone* was astounded.

"B-but bugs are . . ." Gilles stammered.

". . . welcome at the Heartwood Hotel, of course," reminded Mr. Heartwood. "Guests big or small, we welcome all. I believe we are in need of some renovations at the Heartwood, for bug-size rooms. Perhaps, Ms. J, you would be so kind as to offer your consultation?"

"It would be my pleasure," she said.

"Now, Cybele, if you please," said Mr. Heartwood, and the swallow took the stage again and a new song filled the air.

That's when Mona noticed Tilly wasn't there. She wasn't in the dining hall or the lobby either. Where had she gone? It wasn't like Tilly to leave the action. Mona scampered downstairs, but Tilly wasn't in the kitchen or the bedroom either. And then Mona thought of the place *she'd* go if she wanted to be alone, and she began at once up the stairs.

Up, up, up . . . all the way to the stargazing balcony.

It was crisp outside, the moon full and bright in the sky. One animal sat alone on the balcony, staring up at it. Tilly. Her big tail was wrapped around her. She was shivering . . . or maybe . . . Was she crying?

Mona stepped tentatively toward her. "Tilly? Are you okay?"

Tilly looked at Mona. Her fur was wet around her eyes. She sniffled. "Con—congratulations. On your key, I mean."

"Thanks," said Mona, taking a seat beside her, not knowing what Tilly might say next.

"I remember when I first got mine. I was so sad. . . ."

"Sad?" Mona was surprised. "What do you mean?"

"My family . . . I lost them coming here. We were all planning a visit to the hotel, but on the way we were attacked by a coyote. Only I escaped." Tilly gulped back a sob. At last, Mona knew. So that was Tilly's hurt. It *was* a big one.

Tilly continued, "When I found the hotel, Mr. Heartwood took pity on me and offered me a job. He saved me from going back out there. Finally I felt safe. And then you came. I was afraid—afraid you might take my place and I would lose my new home."

Mona couldn't believe it. All this time she thought Tilly didn't like her, but that wasn't the case at all. "But Mr. Heartwood never said—"

"I know," said Tilly. "It's just that I've been

afraid for a long time. Ever since I lost my family. I never used to be so grumpy, you know. . . ."

"I can't even remember my family," said Mona softly. "But I know you. And I know the hotel. This is my family now. I've realized that." She rested her paw on Tilly's.

"Really?" said Tilly. "After everything I've done?"

Mona smiled. "Everyone knows squirrels can be trouble. Wasn't it you who told me that?"

Tilly laughed. And Mona did, too. And then, Mona felt something cold tingle on her nose. She looked up—

Stars were falling. No—not stars, of course. It was snow. Tiny twinkling snowflakes falling from the sky.

It was the First Snow at the Heartwood Hotel. And Mona was certain it wouldn't be her last.

The Pinecone Press

FANCY LODGINGS in FERNWOOD FOREST

"Despite some initial trepidation, I highly recommend the Heartwood Hotel. Guests big or small, it welcomes all. I was, I'm delighted to say, well fed, positively pampered, and snug as a bug!"
—Juniper Jones, *Pinecone Press* Reviewer

The Heartwood Hotel

BUNNY BASEBALL TEAM

ACKNOWLEDGMENTS

It took a big extended family of people to help me with this book, and for that I am forever grateful. Thank you to my mom and dad, my brother and Marie, and my grandparents, who watch over me. Thank you to my friends, in particular my amazing writing group, the Inkslingers (Tanya Lloyd Kyi, Rachelle Delaney, Christy Goerzen, Shannon Ozirny, Lori Sherritt, Maryn Quarless), Lee Edward Fodi, Sara Gillingham, and my writing soul mate, Vikki Vansickle. Thank you to my wonderful, thoughtful, and thorough editors, Rotem Moscovich and Hadley Dyer, and Suzanne Sutherland—and to the incredible teams at Disney-Hyperion and HarperCollins Canada. I am so blessed to work with Stephanie Graegin, who brings Heartwood to life. Thank you to the best agent ever, Emily van Beek, and the best husband ever, Luke Spence Byrd, who is building me my very own Heartwood. And most of all my heart goes to Tiffany Stone and her family. I am forever, forever grateful. (Thank goodness we didn't have to work by messenger jay!)

*Turn the page for a sneak peek at Mona's next
adventure at the Heartwood Hotel!*

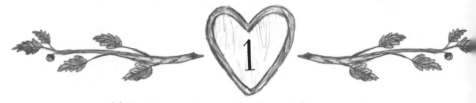
HIBERNATION AT THE HEARTWOOD

Snow fell softly outside the Heartwood Hotel. It was sleepy snow, the kind that took its time to reach the ground. Mona the mouse watched through a small window in the ballroom, leaning against the handle of her dandelion broom. It was so quiet she could almost hear the flakes touch down.

St. Slumber's Supper was finally over. The food was eaten, the music was sung, and gifts were given out by Mr. Heartwood: little sweet-smelling pillows filled with

herbs and lavender, to help the hibernating guests sleep soundly until spring.

And now they had all gone to bed—the groundhog, some toads, turtles, and ladybugs, and so many chipmunks no one could keep track of them.

Even the Higginses, who were hedgehogs, were hibernating. Mr. Higgins was the gardener and Mrs. Higgins was the housekeeper. They weren't needed since only a few non-hibernating guests were booked for the winter months. Most animals in Fernwood Forest, whether they slept through the winter or not, stayed at home.

The Heartwood Hotel was Mona's home now, and she loved it, from the heart carved on the front door to the stargazing balcony on the topmost branches to all of her new friends, like Tilly, the red squirrel maid, and Cybele, the swallow songstress.

Tilly said that the winter season was always really boring, but Mona didn't mind. She had been a maid at the Heartwood only a few months since arriving, wet and afraid, in the fall. But already she had helped save the hotel from wolves and earn it a top review in the *Pinecone Press*. As proud as she was of that, it would be nice to finally rest and roast acorns in the fireplace this winter.

Mona could smell roasted acorns now, their delicious aroma floating up from the kitchen downstairs. The staff were having their own little feast later, and she could hardly wait.

Her stomach grumbled, but she turned her attention back to the task at hand and made a final sweep with her broom, putting the last bits of twine, left over from the gift-giving, in the dust basket. The twine could be used again, so it would need to be taken to the storage room. But the basket was too full for Mona to lift. She'd have to ask Tilly for help.

Mona was just leaving the ballroom to find the squirrel when she heard a voice in the hallway.

"Ah, shadow, what's that you say? A toast to you? Yes, of course! A toast." There was a pause. . . .